MW01138720

The Jerry McNeal Series

Chesapeake Chaos

(A Paranormal Snapshot)

By Sherry A. Burton

Dorry Press

Also by Sherry A. Burton

The Orphan Train Saga
Discovery (book one)
Shameless (book two)
Treachery (book three)
Guardian (book four)
Loyal (book five)

Orphan Train Extras
Ezra's Story

Jerry McNeal Series
Always Faithful (book one)
Ghostly Guidance (book two)
Rambling Spirit (book three)
Chosen Path (book four)
Port Hope (book five)
Cold Case (book six)
Wicked Winds (book seven)
Mystic Angel (book eight)
Uncanny Coincidence (book nine)
Chesapeake Chaos (book ten)
Village Shenanigans (book eleven)
Special Delivery (book twelve)
Spirit of Deadwood (a full-length Jerry McNeal novel)

Clean and Cozy Jerry McNeal Series Collection (Compilations of the standalone Jerry McNeal series)
The Jerry McNeal Clean and Cozy Edition Volume one (books 1-3)
The Jerry McNeal Clean and Cozy Edition Volume two (books 4-6)
The Jerry McNeal Clean and Cozy Edition Volume three (books 7-9)
The Jerry McNeal Clean and Cozy Edition Volume four (books 10-12)

Romance Books (*not clean* - sex and language)
Tears of Betrayal
Love in the Bluegrass
Somewhere In My Dreams
The King of My Heart

Romance Books (clean)
Seems Like Yesterday

"Whispers of the Past" (a short story)

Psychological Thriller
Surviving the Storm (Sex, Language, and Violence)

The Jerry McNeal Series

Chesapeake Chaos
By Sherry A. Burton

The Jerry McNeal Series: Chesapeake Chaos
Copyright 2022

By Sherry A. Burton
Published by Dorry Press
Edited and Formatted by BZHercules.com
Cover by Laura J. Prevost
@laurajprevostphotography
Proofread by Latisha Rich

For more information on the author and her works, please see www.SherryABurton.com

Chapter One

Jerry was jolted from sleep by Gunter's warning growl. As Jerry reached for his gun, a haunting laugh filled the air.

"Too late for that, Mr. McNeal. Too late. Too late," the woman's husky singsong called through the darkness.

Jerry recognized the voice as belonging to Ashley Fabel, the woman who was killed in Port Hope, Michigan, and had haunted Max until he and Gunter had helped locate her remains and give her peace. Well, as much peace as possible until her killer was brought to justice. Either way, the woman was right, as she was already dead. Jerry left the gun on the nightstand and winced as he swung his legs to the side of the bed.

Gunter jumped from the bed and stood between him and the other unearthly spirit.

Ashley clicked her tongue. "If you hadn't been playing in the woods, you wouldn't be suffering with broken ribs."

So much for the accuracy of the spirit network. Jerry glanced around the room, trying to get a fix on

Ashley's precise location. "They are cracked, not broken."

"Broken, shmoken, what's the difference? Even if you do find the killer, how are you going to take him down?"

Jerry pulled his shirt over his head and readjusted the Velcro on the rib brace. When he was satisfied with the placement, he pulled the shirt over his head once more. "If I find him, I'll take him down even if it kills me."

"Yep, that's what they all say until it actually comes to the dying part."

Jerry ran a hand over his head. "What are you doing here, Ashley?"

She sighed an audible sigh. "They sent me."

Jerry flipped on the bedside lamp and waited for his eyes to adjust. Ashley was sitting on the dresser next to the television. He got up and moved to the room's living area, purposely choosing the recliner over the couch so that Ashley wouldn't feel the need to sit beside him. Gunter followed, standing beside his chair. A moment later, Ashley appeared on the couch across from him.

Jerry stifled a yawn and repeated his previous question. "Why are you here?"

"I already told you. They sent me. Before you ask who they are, you already know."

The "they" Ashley was talking about were the other victims of the Hash Mark Killer.

"Yes, I know. What I don't know is why."

"Because they delegated me. Patty wanted to come, but she was voted down, as the others didn't think she'd be able to do the job. Rita wanted to come, but she is too unpredictable. The girl has a real attitude. I swear, if she were alive, I would hook her up with my brother. She and Mario are so much alike that it's not even funny. Those two would either get married or kill each other. Of course, we'll never know which one since Rita is already dead."

Jerry stared at her without blinking. He didn't like talking about Mario Fabel on a good day, much less at three in the morning. "You're giving me a headache. Can we just fast forward to the part where you tell me why you're here?"

Ashley blew out another sigh. "You're boring, Jerry. It's three in the morning, and you're alone in the room with a woman, and all you want to do is talk."

"I prefer my dates to be a bit warmer," Jerry replied dryly.

"Ouch. That smarted. Okay, so what about the woman in the next room? She'd be all over you in a heartbeat. But no, you're pining over a woman who has never even bothered to call."

Jerry sat up straighter in his chair. "You leave April out of this and stay out of my love life."

Ashley snorted. "You're a hoot, Jerry. You don't have a love life to stay out of."

"What are you doing here?" Jerry asked more tersely.

"You don't have to get all testy. I'm just trying to help."

"You could help by letting me sleep. I have a long drive tomorrow."

"Where are you going?"

Ashley was so honed into his situation that Jerry was surprised she didn't already know. "I'm going to Virginia. I think that's where your killer lives." Jerry left off the part that while he felt strongly that the killer lived in Virginia, he had yet to pinpoint the exact location. His hope was that as he grew closer, his feeling would guide him the rest of the way.

"I think you might be right." Her words came out in a whisper.

Jerry leaned forward in his chair, found the position to be uncomfortable, and leaned back once more. "What do you mean you think I'm right?"

Ashley faded in and out.

"Oh, no you don't! You don't get to wake me up, throw out a statement like that, and disappear."

Ashley faded once more, then appeared in full form. Jerry McNeal didn't need a coroner to tell him the cause of death. He merely had to wait and allow the spirit of the victim to show him the atrocities that squelched their life. Though she'd shown him her injuries before, Ashley mostly appeared to him without the bruises and injuries sustained at death.

Ashley now stood in front of him, wearing her death mask. The one that showed what had happened to her in her final hour. He curbed his frustration. "Ashley, you do want to find the person who did that to you, don't you?"

She picked at her sweatshirt, and then her hand went to her throat.

Jerry drummed his fingers on his chair. "You said they sent you. Why you? Do you know something you haven't shared?"

She lowered her gaze. "Maybe."

Jerry struggled to keep his voice calm. "Stop playing games. If you know something that can help me find this guy, just tell me."

She pulled at her shirt once again. "John gave this to me."

They all knew the killer's name probably wasn't John, but it was the one he'd given to her when they'd met. Still, it was a piece of the puzzle she hadn't previously shared. "He gave you the sweatshirt you're wearing?"

"Yes. I was excited because it had a lighthouse. I thought he was being nice. I'm dead because of this stupid shirt."

Jerry peered at the shirt as if seeing it for the first time. He stood, and Gunter jumped to his feet. Jerry bent, lifting his notebook off the table. Flipping back through the pages, he searched for something he remembered Max having said. Finding the page, he stopped and read through what he'd written. *She's wearing a sweatshirt with a lighthouse on it. It doesn't look like one of ours. Something is written on it, but I can't tell what it is.* Jerry peered at the sweatshirt once more. The black and white lighthouse looked familiar. Then again, he'd spent time staring at so many lighthouse images after speaking with Ashley the first time. "Max said there was writing on your shirt."

"There is." Ashley stood and pulled the shirt tight. To the side of the lighthouse, in small print, were the words "Cape Henry Lighthouse." "It's in Virginia Beach, Virginia. When John gave it to me, he said he'd bought it before leaving home and had never worn it. I told him I couldn't take it, but he insisted, telling me not to worry, that he could easily get another. I didn't argue, as I liked the shirt."

While Jerry was excited to have narrowed down the location, he'd been to the area. Just because the guy had access to the lighthouse didn't necessarily mean he lived in Virginia Beach. While some thought Tidewater and Hampton Roads were interchangeable, the area was made up of many large cities that blended into each other and covered a massive land blueprint that housed millions of residents, many of those military transients. Without the help of his gift, finding the killer in an area that size would be like looking for the proverbial needle in a haystack. Even with his gift, Jerry knew he would face challenges, as the energy within the condensed mass would attempt to pull him in many directions. *Easy, McNeal, you're giving in to defeat before you even try.* Jerry pressed his fingers together, rolled his neck, and waited for several breaths before answering. "This is an important piece of the puzzle. Why didn't you tell me this before?"

Ashley shrugged. "I told you he was charming and that I'd allowed myself to agree to have dinner with him. I guess I was too embarrassed to admit that I was murdered because of a stupid shirt. I tried to let Mario know, on account he would know how to deal with the guy, but I couldn't get through to him. I'm kind of glad I couldn't because now the others have a plan."

Jerry frowned. "What kind of plan?"

"Nothing that concerns you. It will only work after the guy is in jail."

"You might have to fight your brother on that one. Mario seems to think he has free rein to take care of the guy once he gets locked up."

Ashley's eyes grew wide. "No! You have to talk to Mario and tell him this is not his fight."

"He's your next of kin. I believe he thinks that makes it his fight." Jerry held up a hand to stop further comments. "How about we wait until after we find your killer to fight that battle?"

She nodded.

"Is there anything else you're keeping from me? Anything, no matter how trivial?"

"No. They wanted me to tell you about the group, but your friend beat me to it."

Jerry sighed. "How long have you ladies known about the connection?"

"Oh, we haven't been keeping that from you. We just put it together ourselves. We had a meeting and were trying to figure out why the killer picked us. We knew there had to be a connection but didn't know what until Rita mentioned posting in the group a few days before she died. Then we all realized that we too had posted."

Jerry had the urge to reach up and close his mouth, as he was fairly certain his jaw had dropped open. "You're telling me you ladies are joining forces on the other side and trying to solve your own murders?"

Ashley laughed. "It's not like you're doing such a hot job of it. We appreciate the effort and all, but it's frustrating when we are all watching, and then you go off on a holiday to save someone else. I mean, finding the kid was cool and all, but it wasn't like she was going anywhere. She could have waited her turn. Then there was your friend. Some friend he turned out to be, punching you when you were down. Rita was mad you didn't take the guy out. She said you missed your opportunity, as no one would have found the guy once the animals got through with him."

Jerry resisted the urge to look for hidden cameras. The only reason he didn't was he knew it was doubtful Ashly's spirit would show up on camera. "How are you watching when I haven't seen or felt you near me?"

"Ghostavision." Ashley laughed. "I don't know who's paying our cable bill, but it's so freaking worth the price. Boy, the things we are able to see."

Jerry shook his head. "Better not let that get out. You're making being dead sound like a good thing."

Ashley rubbed her arms. "It's not."

Jerry waited for her to say more, but she never did. She faded in and out several times before completely disappearing. Gunter sniffed the area Ashley vacated before heading back to the sleeping area. Once there, he jumped onto the bed. Circling several times, he pawed at the covers before lowering to the bed and snorting his contentment.

Just as Jerry decided to tell him to move over so he could join him, his phone chimed, showing a message from Fred. Jerry looked at the time and saw it was just after four. "Does no one ever sleep?" This time, he actually looked for the cameras he was sure were in the room. Not seeing any, he checked the message.

<Fred> *Give me a jingle when you wake up. I want you to take a look at something.*

Jerry sighed and hit reply. *I'm awake.* He waited

for a reply that never came. Instead, two minutes later, there was a light rap on the door. Jerry looked to the bed, half expecting Gunter to bark. When the dog didn't move, Jerry pushed from the chair and walked to the door. Releasing the deadbolt, he opened the door to see Fred standing in the hallway, briefcase in hand. Jerry moved aside to allow him to enter. "What, were you camped out in the parking lot?"

"I have a room on the top floor."

Jerry smiled as he followed the man to the living area. "Penthouse?"

"Nothing but the best." Fred chuckled, then turned serious. "I wanted you to look over Max's contract before I show it to her."

Jerry raised an eyebrow. "Max gets a contract?"

"Of course."

"Why do I suddenly feel like Charlie Brown?"

"What's that supposed to mean?" Fred asked as he sank into the recliner.

"I got a box of business cards. Heck, I didn't even get a company phone. You just printed the cards with my old number."

"Don't forget the cool badge and the gold credit card," Fred reminded him.

The man had a point. The limitless credit card did have its advantages. "How's Stringer liking his lawnmower?" Jerry asked as he took a seat on the couch across from Fred.

Fred narrowed his eyes. "Since I paid for it, I'm assuming he likes it very much."

"That's because you're a good man," Jerry goaded.

"It's because I had no choice," Fred replied as he placed his briefcase in his lap. "If you want a contract, I'd be happy to get you one. I was under the impression you were more inclined to proceed without any reason to stay if you wanted to walk away."

Jerry leaned back against the couch. "I'm alright with the way things are at the moment. That changes, I'll let you know."

Fred handed him a piece of paper. "All the same, I'll need your bank information if you expect to get paid."

Jerry eyed the paper. "I'm surprised you don't already have it."

Fred smiled a sly smile. "I do, but this makes it official."

Jerry checked his phone, jotted down his information, and then handed Fred the slip.

"Aren't you curious about how much we're paying you?" Fred asked, placing the paper in his briefcase.

Jerry shook his head. "If the endless credit card is any indication, I figure I'll be okay with the number."

"It comes with a company car if you're

interested."

Jerry shook his head. "I like my ride."

"Let me know if you change your mind. I can tell you it's a good deal more than we're paying the girl," Fred replied, passing Max's contract to Jerry.

Jerry lifted the cover sheet and blew out a whistle. "That's quite a number for a twelve-year-old."

Fred nodded. "You know an adult who can do the same job? Let me know who it is, and I'll sign them instead."

Jerry shook his head. "There's no one like Max."

Fred sat back and nodded at the paper. "That should be enough to allow April the freedom to quit her job and travel with Max as needed."

Jerry continued to read over the contract. "It says here their expenses will be covered anytime Max is needed. That money is going to go a long way in the town they live in."

"Maybe they will decide to move."

"Doubtful. April and Max like where they live. It's safe."

Fred worried his fingertips together. "Did either of them ever tell you about why they left Detroit?"

Jerry nodded. "A little. Sounds like the guy April married was a real jerk."

Fred's voice turned serious. "I have another name for the guy. A real piece of work. Randy about killed April. Probably would have if Max hadn't called 911."

Jerry felt a sudden rage welling inside. "How do you know?"

"I heard the 911 call. Let me know if you want to listen to it, but I promise it will break your heart. The man was beating on April. I'll save you the particulars, but it was bad. Real bad. Max started screaming into the phone that he was going to kill her mom. The guy realized she'd called for help and turned on Max."

The thought of anyone hurting either Max or her mom made Jerry's blood boil. "Max hinted about some things, but I didn't know the extent of it. Where's this Randy guy now?"

"Still in Detroit. He did a little time for what he did, but he's out now. Don't worry, we've got eyes on him. I already told you. We take care of our family."

Jerry returned the contract to Fred. "Mr. Jefferies, if you keep this up, people will start thinking you're a good guy."

Fred shook his head. "Please don't go spreading rumors. Something like that gets out, and I'll never live it down."

Jerry winked. "Don't worry, Boss. Your secret is safe with me."

Chapter Two

Now that the contract review was out of the way, the two men sat enjoying a cup of coffee as Jerry told him about Ashley's visit. Fred took it all in, waiting until Jerry finished speaking before commenting. "Too bad she didn't come forth with that bit of information from the beginning."

"Could've, would've, should've; nothing to be done about it now," Jerry replied, using one of his grandmother's phrases.

Fred leaned back in his chair and crossed one leg over the other. "True. It's easy to cast blame. Look at the rest of the case. It took April poring through the Facebook pages to find a connection to the women. The police should have figured that out and probably would have if they knew the women's disappearances had been connected. We need to make sure not to underestimate this guy. He's smart."

Jerry nodded his agreement. "It isn't the police's fault. There was no body, therefore no crime. As far as they knew, the girls had simply disappeared. Let's face it, we probably still wouldn't know there was a serial killer if not for the spirits reaching out. If not for Patti and Ashley, I wouldn't have asked Seltzer to see if there were any more."

"I shudder to think how many other bodies he could have stacked up if not for that gift of yours," Fred agreed.

Jerry squirmed in his seat. "I wasn't fishing for a compliment."

"Didn't think you were. I was just stating the obvious. Speaking of which, I think we should bring Max and April along."

Jerry wasn't so sure. "For what purpose? Max already did her part. We have a sketch of the guy."

Fred held firm. "From what you've told me, she's helped you on more than one case. Having a second pair of eyes couldn't hurt."

"Twelve-year-old eyes," Jerry reminded him. "Max can do what she does from the safety of her own home."

Fred jutted his thumb toward the wall that separated their room. "Listen, ultimately, it will be your call, but I think we should keep them close until the killer is caught. The last thing we need is either one of them trying to help with the case without our okay. To our knowledge, the killer has never killed on his home turf. But he did kill a woman in that sleepy little town where Max and April live. Besides, don't you think they deserve a trip to the beach?"

Jerry had to admit the man had a point, at least about keeping them close. "It's too chilly to get in the water."

Fred laughed. "They live in Michigan. The ocean will feel like bathwater. Besides, we'll put them in a hotel at the waterfront with a pool. We'll get you a room right next door if you want."

Jerry did like the idea of being able to keep an eye on Max and April when he wasn't working. "Who's going to keep an eye on them when I'm on the job?"

"Barney and I will stay on the same floor. Heck, we'll rent the whole floor if it will make you feel better. I'll even bring someone in to keep an eye on them when we can't."

Jerry didn't have any bad feelings about them coming. The least he could do was to present it to Max. If she got any bad vibes, they would yank the whole plan and send her and April back to Michigan. He blew out a sigh. "Okay. But you need to get them there."

Fred cocked his head. "You don't want them to ride with you?"

Jerry shook his head. "It's not how I work. I need to be able to listen to my feeling and let it draw me in. Maybe I will lock on to something as soon as I arrive, or it might take a couple of days to find what I'm looking for. Either way, I can't do what I do if I am worried about them getting too close to the killer."

"Okay, we'll make arrangements to get them there safely."

Jerry nodded his agreement. While he would love nothing more than to spend more time with Max and April, a part of him was worried. What if they expected more of him than he was able to give? *Who are you saving your feelings for, McNeal?* Just as the thought came to him, he remembered what Ashley had said about pining for the wrong woman. He wavered for a second, then pushed off the temptation to tell Fred he'd reconsidered. *Get a grip, McNeal. This isn't a family outing – you're searching for a serial killer.*

Fred looked him over. "Are you alright? We could fly you in and get you something to drive when you get there."

Nothing a few weeks of sleep won't cure. Jerry kept the thought to himself. "I'm good. I just need to get there and get this done."

"Okay, McNeal, you're the boss." Fred winked. "Don't let that go to your head."

Jerry smiled. "I wouldn't think of it."

Fred drained his coffee cup. "Want me to hang around to help you go over the contract with them?"

Jerry's smile widened. "We both know how legal it is to enter a contract with a minor."

"Don't forget we are including the mother in on the deal. You and I both know it wouldn't hold up in court, but we are not out to screw them over. Your girl Max has a gift that would be useful in many narratives. While she would probably be willing to do this for free just for the benefits, I would prefer to get her settled into the family. How many twelve-year-olds do you know that don't have to worry about what they want to be when they grow up?"

Fred had a point. Jerry knew the gift well enough to know that Max's abilities would only get more refined with age. Best to allow her the opportunity to utilize her skill instead of having her spend her life questioning it. Jerry nodded. "You're right. I'll make sure they both know how fortunate Max is to get an opportunity like this."

Fred pushed from the chair, and Jerry eased his way off the couch. From his spot on the bed, Gunter opened his eyes, watching the process. Jerry chuckled.

Fred lifted an eyebrow. "Did I miss something?"

Jerry nodded toward the bed. "That dog gets more sleep than I do, and he's dead. My granny had trouble sleeping. I can remember her walking the halls long into the night. I once asked her why she didn't sleep, and she told me there'd be time enough to sleep after she was dead. Maybe that's what she was talking about." Then again, she'd also told him spirits didn't need sleep. Jerry decided to keep that tidbit to himself.

Fred looked toward the bed, and Jerry knew the

man was trying his darndest to see the ghostly visitor. Finally, he sighed his disappointment and returned his focus to Jerry. "The contract's on the table. You lay it all out. If they are agreeable, have them sign it. I'll see that your ride is brought to the front of the building so you don't have so far to walk."

"Sounds like a plan," Jerry agreed.

It didn't take long for Jerry to pack, mainly because he hadn't brought anything into the Navy Lodge. Except for the items Barney had brought to his hospital room, everything Jerry owned was still inside his Durango.

He'd just finished triple-checking everything when he heard a knock on the door.

Gunter barked an excited yip. Jumping from the bed, he ran across the room and shoved his head through the door. Jerry heard giggles on the other side and knew it had to be Max.

"Okay, boy, in or out. I can't open the door with your head sticking through it." Gunter withdrew his head, and Jerry pulled the door open.

Max's face beamed with childhood curiosity as she dropped to her knee, greeting the dog. "That is so cool he can do that."

Jerry grinned. "You should see him when we're going down the highway. He doesn't need me to roll down the window. He just sticks his head straight through the glass."

Max's eyes sparkled. "That is super cool!"

Jerry looked over her shoulder. "Is your mother coming?"

"Yeah, she'll be here in a minute. She's double-checking to make sure we didn't leave anything in the room. I don't know why she bothers. I've already checked it twice."

"It's a grown-up thing. You'll understand one day. I already checked my room three times." Jerry heard a door shut and looked to see April coming toward him fresh as the dawn of day. He sucked in a breath. She'd curled her hair and was wearing just enough makeup to make her eyes pop. He smiled. "You look nice."

She blushed, adding even more color to her cheeks. "It's amazing what a good night's sleep will do to a person. How about you? Did you sleep well?"

Until about three a.m. Jerry decided not to worry them about Ashley's visit. "I slept well when I slept. I've been up for a while. Fred and I had an early meeting."

April frowned. "Nothing bad, I hope."

"No, as a matter of fact, I think you will find what we discussed very good."

She raised an eyebrow. "Oh?"

Jerry motioned them to the living area. "Have a seat. I have something to discuss with you."

They sat on the couch and watched as he pulled

the contract Fred had left with him from the table. He sat beside Max and held the contract for them to see. "This is for Max, but since she can't legally enter into a contract as a minor, it is mostly a formality. Basically, it tells you what they are offering and all that goes with the job."

April took the paper he offered. "Who are they?"

Jerry blew out a sigh. "To be honest, I am not sure the exact name of the agency. It's a part of the government, but Fred is a bit closed-lipped on the details."

"And you feel comfortable not knowing who you are working for?"

She sounded as skeptical as Seltzer. Jerry knew he wasn't showing good business sense, but he also knew his feeling would have told him if he was being duped. "They are the good guys, and I can do my thing, so it works for me. If you want to know more, I understand. I can call Fred and have him come down to answer your questions."

Max took the contract from her mother. She closed her eyes and held the papers to her chest. Opening her eyes once more, she handed them back to April. "It's okay, Mom. Jerry's right, it's a good thing."

April smiled. "Okay, Max, if you say so." April lifted the cover sheet and clutched her chest. "Is this what they are paying her?"

Jerry grinned. "Caught me by surprise too."

Max leaned in and started at the number. "Whoa! Wait until I tell Chloe!"

April wagged a finger at her. "You'll do no such thing. No one needs to know you're making this kind of money."

"Not even Chloe?"

April shook her head. "Especially not Chloe. Poor kid would never be able to make this kind of money even straight out of college."

Jerry nodded to the forms, then back to April. "The idea is for them to pay enough to allow you to quit your job. That way, if Max is needed, you're not getting in trouble for taking time off."

April frowned. "What about school?"

"The contract states they will do their best to work around her schedule. It also promises to hire a private teacher to home-school her if the need arises. I don't think it will come to that, but it is there if it does."

April looked to where he was pointing. "It seems they've thought of everything."

Jerry met her eye. "You can always say no."

Max's eyes grew wide. "You won't, will you, Mom?"

April sighed. "No, Max. I would never hold you back from an opportunity like this. So, we sign it. Then what? When does she start?"

"Immediately. I'm heading to Virginia. Fred thinks it would be good to have you guys come down too."

Max dropped to the floor, running her hands through Gunter's fur. "Did you hear that, boy? We're going to Virginia with you."

Jerry shook his head. "You're not going with me. I'll meet you there."

Max drew her brows together. "Why can't we come with you?"

"I would love for you to, but I need to focus on the killer."

Max grabbed the pen and signed her name on the paper. "There, I work with you. Now I can come along."

Jerry knew he would have trouble with this part of the plan. "Not this time, Max."

April touched Max's arm. "Max, if you're old enough to have a job this important, you are old enough to listen."

"If I'm old enough to have a job, I'm old enough to help," Max countered.

Jerry looked to Gunter for help. The dog didn't seem inclined to get involved as he just sat there watching the exchange. *Thanks for nothing, dog.*

Gunter answered with a yawn. Jerry ran a hand over his head. He was used to dealing with adults, not a kid who thought she was an adult. It didn't help that Max was more of an adult than some adults he'd dealt with. "Listen, Max, the company is bringing you to Virginia because they want you to help."

"Then it's you who doesn't want me?" The wounded look on Max's face was nearly enough to make him reconsider.

Jerry firmed his chin. "That's not fair, Max. You know what the gift is like. You also know that sometimes you must concentrate. Remember when we were in the room, and Fiona was telling you what the killer looked like? I stayed quiet so you could do your job. We are not going to Virginia to find a dead body in a cemetery. We are going to find a killer. I need to use all of my senses. I can't do that if I'm distracted. I promise I will bring you in if and when I need you. But for now, I need you to let me do my job. Okay?"

Max nodded. "Okay, Jerry."

He could tell she still wasn't happy with the arrangement, but it didn't sound as if she would give him any more grief over his decision. Gunter, on the other hand, gave him a look that said, *You have everything you ever wanted right here in front of you, and you're just letting it slip away. What are you afraid of?* Then again, he could just be hearing the thoughts racing in his own head.

Chapter Three

It unnerved Jerry to watch Max and April climb into the back of Fred's town car. He didn't have a feeling that something bad would happen; he just didn't like seeing them move away from him. Jerry lowered his window and started to call out to tell them he'd changed his mind, but then the door closed, the brake lights went out, and the car pulled away. Jerry followed the town car out of the parking lot, got caught by the light at the gate, and watched as the vehicle got sucked up in traffic until he could no longer single it out. Jerry heaved a sigh.

Gunter cocked his head, looking at him as if saying, *You had your chance and blew it.*

Jerry shrugged off the accusation. "Quit looking at me like that. We have a job to do and can't do it if we're distracted."

"How long are you going to use that excuse?"

The voice was croaky, and for a moment, Jerry thought it was Gunter who'd spoken. He heard a snicker and realized the voice had come from the back seat. He looked in the mirror and saw Granny smiling back at him.

She cleared her throat and cracked a wrinkled smile. When she next spoke, she sounded more like herself. "Ha, had you fooled there for a moment."

The light turned green. Jerry pressed on the gas, wheeling into traffic as he answered, "I thought I'd finally lost it."

Granny motioned Gunter to the back and accepted some K-9 kisses before appearing in the seat beside Jerry. "And yet you believe it is perfectly normal to talk to the spirit of your dead granny."

Jerry shrugged. "Seems so to me."

She slapped her hand on her knee. "Good, I trained you right."

Jerry weaved his way through traffic and merged onto the interstate. "I guess so."

"Too good, maybe."

Jerry detected a tinge of regret in her words. "How so?"

"Because you seem to be more comfortable being alone."

"I'm not alone." To prove his point, Jerry worked his way into the HOV lane reserved for two or more occupants.

She laughed a hearty laugh. "I can see you trying to talk your way out of that ticket. 'But, officer, I'm not alone. I was talking to the ghost of my dead grandmother.'"

"I wouldn't say ghost. I'd say spirit. And then I'd point to you, and you'd show yourself and scare the crap out of him, and he would walk away without another word."

Granny clapped her hands together, giggling her ghostly delight. "Go faster. I can't wait to get pulled over."

Jerry shook his head at her childish antics – something that was a holdover from her life. For as long as he could remember, his grandmother was the first to let go of what others perceived as normal in order to have fun. His mother often chastised the woman for refusing to act her age, for which his grandmother would deem her a fuddy-duddy. Sometimes his mother would stand her ground, but most often, she would blow out an exasperated sigh and go on as to how Granny wasn't setting a good example for Jerry. "Let's forget I suggested it. And if I get pulled over, you'd better not disappear."

Granny clicked her tongue. "Oh poo, and here I thought we'd found a new game to play."

"Making police officers question their mental status is not a game I care to play," Jerry replied dryly.

Granny stretched her legs and propped them on the dashboard in front of her.

"Don't ride like that. That airbag goes off, and you're as good as dead." Jerry realized what he'd said and shook his head. "It's easy to forget you're already dead when you seem so full of life."

"It's alright, Jerry. I'm as alive as you want me

to be."

Sitting here having this conversation, Jerry was glad he hadn't agreed to let Max and her mother ride with him.

"Oh no, you don't. You don't get to pin that on me."

That she'd heard his thoughts was no surprise; they'd often communicated without words even when the woman was alive. "I wouldn't be able to do my job if they were with me."

"Or you and Max could work together and find the killer even faster."

Jerry glanced at her. "You don't know that to be the case."

"And you don't know that it's not," she retorted. "You're running. Just like you've always done. You ran to the Marines, and when you couldn't control things there, you ran. You ran from that woman. What was her name? Holly? And now you are running from Max and her mother."

Jerry ran his hand over his head. The only reason his grandmother even knew about Holly was he'd allowed her into his thoughts. "I didn't run from Holly. She was leaving town to be with her family."

"What would you expect her to do? She'd nearly lost her life and left her daughter without a mother. She was scared and didn't have anything keeping her in Pennsylvania. How do you know you couldn't have changed her mind?"

Jerry resisted the urge to tell his grandmother to get out of his head. Instead, he tightened his grip on the steering wheel. "In case you haven't noticed, I'm no longer in Pennsylvania."

"No, but you have a second chance at happiness. Max and April care for you very much."

"And I them. And that's where it stops."

"Why, Jerry? Why does it have to stop? You're nearly thirty-three years old. Don't you think you deserve some happiness? You don't have to go through life alone."

Gunter placed his paws on the center console and yawned a squeaky yawn.

"I'm not alone. I have Gunter." Jerry reached his hand to calm him. "And in case you haven't noticed, you're upsetting him."

"Hmph. The dog would welcome them into the family, and you know it. He's already shown his loyalty to both Max and her mother."

For lack of a better response, Jerry started laughing.

"What's so funny?"

"You remind me of Mom."

"I should. I'm her mother."

"No, I mean she used to do the same thing. She would wait until we were in the car and I couldn't get away to talk about stuff she knew I wouldn't want to talk about."

"You mean the birds and the bees?"

Jerry nodded. "That too. She knew what she was doing too, because she'd always wait until we were going fast enough where I knew it wasn't safe to jump out."

"Your mother never drove a car a day in her life. If you were going fast, it was because you were driving. Why not just stop and get out?"

"Same as now, I always had someplace I needed to be." He was feeling calmer now. "I like Max. She's a great kid. I like April too."

"Why do I feel there's a 'but' at the end of that sentence?"

Jerry pictured April and how her soft curls danced along her shoulders when she moved her head. The image blurred and gave way to Holly and how she had looked at him when he saved her from sure death. He'd been taken with her even before they'd actually met and was surprised when she was the woman he'd rescued. But that was before he started spending time with April. Thinking of April made him smile. He really did enjoy their time together. When he was a kid, he'd had a magic eight ball that he could turn over and ask a question. He would then concentrate as he shook the ball before turning it over to see the answer displayed on a floating triangle. Most of the time, he was greeted with *don't know*. Or *ask again later*. He pictured the ball in his hands, shook it and was greeted with the same response from his childhood. Jerry shrugged and read the response out loud. "I just don't know."

His grandmother reached a hand across and patted him on the arm. "You'll figure it out, Jerry, and it will be a lucky woman who gets you when you do. Whatever you decide, don't worry about Max. The dog will protect her just as he does you. And, Jerry, I want to remind you of something."

"What's that, Granny?"

"You are worthy of love. Don't be afraid to take that next step because you don't think you deserve something good."

Jerry tightened his grip on the wheel. Before he could respond, she disappeared.

Gunter reappeared in the now vacated seat. The dog sniffed the chair, then lowered and lay with his head on the console, looking at Jerry as if to say, *Don't worry. If you don't get your act together, you'll always have me.*

***

Much to Jerry's relief, the rest of the drive proved uneventful and devoid of any further spiritual advice. Even the drive from Williamsburg to Newport News, Virginia was less congested than he remembered, mainly because they had added extra lanes to help with traffic flow. Once in Newport News, the highway expanded even more, with drivers spreading out and increasing their speed – each obviously eager to cross the distance before the lanes merged and forced them to funnel into the

Hampton Roads Tunnel. The closer he got to the tunnel, the more the feeling pulled at him, drawing him in. Jerry would have gladly followed that pull if not for the fact that traffic ahead of him was now moving at a snail's pace. Jerry slowed and closed the distance to the SUV ahead of him. A lot had changed since he was last in the area. Traffic was not one of those things. While it looked as if the city was working to ease traffic flow by adding more lanes along with a second tunnel to help alleviate congestion, a project that size would take years to complete. A shame, since he would now have to bide his time inching forward with every other impatient soul who found themselves on the road this day. Even more frustrating was that every nerve in his body now told him that the killer was somewhere on the other side of the tunnel.

The SUV in front of him rolled to a stop, and the lane next to him did the same. *Great. Gridlock. Probably a wreck in the tunnel.* Jerry waited several moments, then switched into park.

Gunter stood, craning his neck to see out the front window.

Jerry stretched, wincing against the pain in his ribcage, then called to Gunter, "Might as well go back to sleep. I think we're going to be here a while."

Gunter moved from the front seat to the back and forward again before finally disappearing. An instant later, he appeared outside the Durango, walking the line of cars in the left lane and leaving ghostly markings along their right rear tires. Jerry wondered if any of the dog's earthly counterparts ever sniffed the tires and questioned what they were smelling.

The rear window of a dark blue Blazer slid down, and a small hand pushed through the opening, waving the dog closer with a single finger. Gunter raced to the SUV, placed his paws on the door, and proceeded to lick the fingers as his tail fanned his delight. The driver turned to look over their shoulder. The hand pulled back inside, and the window glided shut. Not one to be easily deterred, Gunter disappeared, reappearing a second later inside the vehicle. That the driver didn't run from the SUV screaming told Jerry the person was unaware of their unearthly passenger. The child in the backseat was well aware, as they had their hands buried in the K-9's fur as he smothered the child with eager kisses. Jerry smiled. Oh, to be a fly on the ceiling listening to the goings-on in that vehicle.

Traffic began to move forward. As Jerry reached the tunnel entrance, Gunter reappeared in the front seat with the barest hint of a K-9 smile.

Jerry glanced at Gunter. "You're looking mighty pleased with yourself."

Gunter lifted a lip to widen the smile.

Jerry chuckled. "Poor kid's probably going to get

in trouble for telling lies."

Gunter's smile disappeared.

Jerry scratched him behind the ear. "It's okay, boy. I'm sure the mom will strike it up as simple boredom."

As they reached what felt like the bottom of the tunnel, Jerry drew back his hand and placed it on the steering wheel. "I envy childish innocence. The energy in that line of traffic was palpable. I believe I picked up on every foul mood out there. Man, I hate crowds. It's going to be interesting to see how things play out here. I've seen a dozen white vans since we left Williamsburg. How are we going to find the right one? For all I know, one of those could have been the killer." Only Jerry knew that was not the case as the pull continued to draw him forward.

Chapter Four

Jerry should have known better than to arrive in Norfolk at rush hour. The traffic heading out of the city felt like an ill-planned stock car race, with everyone vying for the best position. Jerry wasn't the only one on heightened alert. Gunter sat in the passenger seat, watching the road ahead.

The dash lit up, announcing a call from Fred. Jerry pressed the button to answer. "Hello."

"Just wanted to let you know we're here."

"Where's here?"

"We've secured a house in Chesapeake. It's in a quiet area close to the North Carolina border. The house has plenty of bedrooms, a pool, and is in an upscale neighborhood not known for short-term rentals."

Jerry liked that the house was in a neighborhood, as that lessened the probability of people randomly driving past the house. "Nice touch."

"I thought you'd approve. How about you? What's your status?"

"I'm in the area. Don't know what I was thinking arriving during rush hour. The traffic is even worse than I remember."

"I didn't realize you'd been here before."

"Never stationed here, but I came up a few times when I was at Camp Lejeune."

"Anything tickling your radar?"

"Everything, but nothing solid just yet. Even if I had the guy in my sights, he would probably be able to slip away."

"I was thinking the same thing. Maybe we'll have to bring the guy to us."

Jerry rolled his neck. "How do you suggest we do that?"

"By offering him something he doesn't know he wants."

"I've already told you, April is not to get involved."

"April's not his type. I have someone else in mind."

"Who?"

"Susie Richardson."

Jerry shook his head at the screen. "Too risky. She is the only one that can positively identify the guy."

"Which is why she's perfect. We can bring her in and have her drop a few key posts in the group and sit back and wait."

"What's Susie say about it?"

"Heck, it was her idea. You'd think she'd be happy with the deal she has, but according to the woman we have watching her, she is behaving like a caged animal. She's been honing her psychic skills with your friend Savannah and has also been taking kickboxing lessons. The guy won't have a chance."

Jerry drummed his fingers on the wheel. "Not yet. We'll keep that in our back pocket. Let me see if I can get a bead on this guy first."

"Do you really think you'll be able to find him?"

"I can feel him. He's close, but the energy in this town is chaotic at the moment. Let me see what happens after traffic dies down."

"Okay, we'll do it your way for now. I'll send you the address of where we are, and you can at least get settled."

The dash showed a second call coming in. Jerry recognized the number as belonging to Savannah. "Hey, I have another call. Text me the address, and I'll head that way." Jerry pressed to switch calls. "What's up, lady?"

"Nothing."

It was a simple word, but the tone in which it was said was anything but simple. "It doesn't sound like nothing."

"I just wanted to know why I'm good enough to help your friends but not good enough to be involved with the good stuff?"

Jerry glanced at Gunter, then shrugged at the dash. "I assure you I have no idea what you're talking about."

"You keep sending me people to train to use their abilities."

"That's right. I thought you enjoyed it. I didn't realize there was a problem. If there is, I can stop giving out your name."

"It's not a problem. It just kind of hurt when Susie told me she was heading to Virginia to help find the killer. Then when I checked in with Max, I found out she is already there. I'm the one training them. How come I wasn't asked to come along? Don't I have anything to offer?"

Jerry could understand her frustration. He was fairly irritated himself at the moment. He worked to keep his anger under control. "None of this is my doing. I was just on the phone with my contact, and it was the first I'd heard about using Susie. I didn't even know the plan was a go until you told me."

"Does that mean I can come?"

You've got just as much right as anyone else, Jerry thought.

"Cool. Wait until I tell Alex."

"Wait, tell Alex what?"

"That I'm going to Virginia."

"I don't think I said that out loud." He glanced at Gunter. "You didn't hear me say that out loud, did you?"

Gunter yawned. Jerry knew that was his way of saying, *You got yourself into this.*

"I need to get a bathing suit. Maybe I should wait

until I get to Virginia. They probably have a better selection this time of year. It's a beach town. I'm sure they sell them year-round. Should I drive or fly? No, I'll probably drive. I can pack more that way."

"You should stay home. We're trying to catch a killer, not having a beach party."

"I know it's not a party, but Max said there's a pool. Surely we will have some time to swim. I can stay at the house. Right? Max said there is plenty of room."

Jerry realized he was driving by pure instinct. He further realized that now that she'd made up her mind, Savannah would not be reasoned with. "Listen, I have to go so I can plug in the address. Hang tight at the house and I will have Fred send a driver for you."

"Someone's going to drive me to Virginia?"

"No, to the airport to catch your plane."

"I haven't made reservations."

"You don't have to. We'll take care of that on our end. Just sit tight and I'll let you know when you can expect someone."

"Will they pay for my luggage?"

"I'm sure they will not mind if you have more than one bag. Got to go. I'll talk to you soon." Jerry pulled up the text from Fred and read the address to the Durango's Alexa. He thought about calling Fred and telling him that Savannah was coming but decided it could wait until he got there, mostly because he was too pissed off to talk to the man. Once past the Greenbriar exit, traffic started to ease. By the time he got to 168, traffic had thinned even more. As Jerry started over the Albemarle and Chesapeake Canal overpass, the hair on the back of his neck stood on end. He checked the cars in front of him, expecting to see a white van. There wasn't one. He looked in his rearview mirror. *Nothing.* He snuck a glance toward Gunter. The dog's ears quivered as if he, too, felt the pull. "Do you think maybe it's just because we're getting close to Max?"

Gunter leaned forward, placing his paws on the dash. Peering ahead, he answered in K-9 woofs.

"You know, it would be easier if you could talk." Gunter grew quiet. Jerry sighed when he realized that he half expected the dog to answer. By the time he got to the road sign that announced the restaurant choices for exit 11B, his internal radar was screaming.

What am I missing? Jerry scanned the area and saw nothing but trees. He focused on the road in front of him and then glanced in the rearview mirror. Nothing looked out of place, yet his psychic radar was screaming for him to pay attention. A car passed him on the left and sounded its horn. Jerry checked his speed, realized he was driving way under the speed limit, and pressed on the gas. Gunter emitted a grumbling yawn and lowered from the dash. Jerry turned on his blinker, thinking to take the Mt.

Pleasant Road exit, then realized the need to react was no longer there. He switched off his turn signal, passed both 11A and 11B, and drove the short distance to 10B, his original Hanbury Road exit. He took the off-ramp, drove past Hanbury Village, then took a right onto Hillwell Road.

Gunter moved to the second-row seat and paced back and forth. His excited whines morphed into full-fledged barks as Jerry turned left onto Mill Stone Road.

Gunter continued his serenade as Jerry pulled into a long driveway and double-checked the numbers on a small brick structure near the end of the driveway. *Weird, why does it feel like there's a whole staff in there?* He chuckled. *I've been on the road too long.* He crept past the structure, half expecting someone to stop him, but continued forward when no one did. As he rounded a bend in the driveway, the house came into view. Jerry blew out a long whistle. As wide as it was tall, the house would easily sell for a million dollars, if not more. If not for the fact that Fred's town car was parked in the driveway among several SUVs, Jerry would have thought he had the wrong address.

Gunter's ears twitched.

"Looks like we're in trouble, dude. Max and April are never going to want to leave this place."

Gunter appeared in the front passenger seat, wagging his tail and barking his enthusiasm.

Jerry pulled up beside Fred's town car and stared at the car for a moment before shutting off his engine and getting out of his Durango. He stretched, felt the pain in his ribs, and regretted the action. The front door opened.

Fred stepped out, welcoming him with a smile. Gunter ran to him, tail wagging and sniffing places that had the man unconsciously shifting from foot to foot.

While Gunter was obviously excited to have arrived, Jerry was less enthused. Jerry's jaw twitched. "You need to go back inside."

Fred's head jerked up, and the smile vanished. "Excuse me."

"I'm not all that anxious to talk to you alone right now."

Fred raised an eyebrow but continued his approach, waiting until he'd nearly reached Jerry before he spoke. "I guess that means you know Susie is on her way."

"I thought we agreed to wait."

"We did."

The front door opened, and Max and April stepped outside. Max started toward them. April must have sensed the tension as she called her back. Jerry was glad when they both walked to the far end of the porch and sat on the porch swing as Gunter ran to greet them.

Jerry turned his attention back to Fred. "I don't

like being played."

Fred held his hands up. "No one is playing you."

"Then why are you bringing her in when we already decided to wait?"

"The ball was already in motion before we spoke. You said yourself that you aren't sure if you can get a bead on this guy. Don't you think it would be best if she is here when we need her?"

Jerry narrowed his eyes. "You mean 'if'?"

Fred rocked back on his heels. "No, I mean when. You're forgetting she is the only one who can identify the guy."

Jerry sighed his acceptance. "Are you sure the location is safe?"

The smile returned to Fred's face. "Probably not a safer location in the area. We use this when we have very important guests. The house is fully wired and there are security measures in place even I don't know about. Nothing moves on this property without someone having eyes on it. Unless our guy is some kind of Rambo, these measures are all overkill, but if we have them at our disposal, why not use them?"

Jerry thought about reminding Fred that if anything went wrong, it was on him, but that went without saying. Besides, if things weren't as they seemed, Jerry would be the first to know. He looked to the porch where Max sat petting Gunter. Okay, probably the second to know. That Max was so relaxed eased his own tension.

Fred nodded toward the Durango. "How was the drive? Did you pick up on anything along the way?"

Jerry rubbed the back of his neck. "Something. Not sure what just yet."

"Want to talk about it?"

Jerry shook his head. "Nope."

A frown tugged at Fred's mouth. "Okay."

Jerry cracked a smile. "Don't go moping. I'm not holding anything back. It's just too early to say what I felt." *Mostly because I don't know just yet.* "Oh, and I need you to send someone to pick up Savannah."

Fred cocked an eyebrow. "You're asking for help?"

"If Susie gets involved, I want Savannah here. I told her you would send a driver for her and arrange transportation." Taking Fred's non-answer as an answer, Jerry pushed the button to lift the back hatch and started toward the back of the Durango.

Fred stopped him as he got ready to lift his duffel bag. "Unless you've magically healed in the last few hours, I'd leave that to someone else."

Jerry nodded his agreement. "Okay, but I'd like to keep eyes on my gun bag."

Fred reached around him, eyeing him as he lifted the bag. "Speaking of Rambo."

Jerry shrugged. "It's not like I have anyplace else to keep them."

"Maybe you should think about putting down roots." Fred hefted the bag to his shoulder and looked toward the porch. "I don't know what those two mean to you, but from the way you protect them, I'd say it's a lot. I know both of them are rather fond of you. They talked about you the whole way here."

"It's probably just hero syndrome. I helped Max. It's normal for them to think it's more than what it is."

"All I know is what I saw and heard. The way I see it, they need you as much as you need them," Fred countered.

Fred's comment tugged at his heart. "Who says I need them?"

"We all need someone, McNeal." Fred grabbed Jerry's duffel bag with his free hand and started for the house without another word.

Jerry picked up the smallest bag and lowered the hatch.

Max raced from the porch and took the bag from him. "I'll put this in your room for you." Gunter joined her as she followed Fred into the house.

Jerry walked to where April still sat on the porch swing. Though she smiled, her demeanor seemed hesitant, almost as if she were scared of him. Jerry frowned. "Is everything alright?"

She nodded. "Yes, why wouldn't it be? Can you believe this place? It's absolutely amazing."

Though she was saying all the right things,

something felt off. He sat beside her and she stiffened. Jerry lifted his arm, intending to place it behind her on the swing. April flinched. He recognized the reflex as someone who was used to being hit and slowly lowered his arm, placing his hand on his thigh. "I'm sorry. I didn't mean…"

April cut him off. "No, I'm sorry. I saw you talking to Fred, and you seemed upset. It's been my experience that if a man is upset, he hits."

"Not all men," Jerry replied softly and smiled when April placed her hand on top of his.

Chapter Five

Jerry opened his eyes and stared at the clock in disbelief. *7:42* He couldn't remember the last time he'd slept past seven. Heck, he couldn't recall the last time he'd slept past five. He looked for Gunter, surprised not to see him. *Max.* Though the dog's loyalties were to him, it was obvious Max ranked right up there with him. He wondered where April fit into the mix, then recalled what Max had said about their bike ride. Gunter hadn't come to protect her; he'd gone to protect April. Did that mean something, or was Gunter simply acting because he knew Max was afraid? It didn't matter. What did matter was when it came to protecting those Jerry cared about, Gunter had done so without fail.

Jerry took a quick shower and had just replaced his rib brace when his phone chimed, alerting him to an email. He finished dressing and checked his phone, his jaw twitching when he saw who the email was from. *Holly.* Jerry sat in the chair, staring at the phone, debating if he should read the email or simply swipe it away. He had yearned to hear from Holly for so long, and now he just wasn't sure, as it seemed his heart was leading him in another direction. There was a knock on the door. Jerry stuffed his phone into his pocket. *Sheesh, McNeal, you're acting like a kid who just got caught with his hand in the cookie jar.* He walked to the door and opened it to see Max standing there with Gunter by her side.

Max took one look at his face, looked at the pocket that hid the phone, and frowned. "Mom wanted me to ask if you wanted some breakfast."

While Max couldn't read minds, she was very skilled at reading him and had picked up on Holly once before. Jerry started to explain and decided against it. How could he explain what he didn't know? He smiled. "I would love breakfast."

Max turned without further comment. Gunter stayed at her side as Jerry followed her down the hall.

"How'd you sleep?" Jerry asked.

"Good."

"Is your room nice?"

"Yes." Max's one-word answers confirmed that she was upset.

Jerry stepped up beside her just before she started downstairs. "Okay, Max, what's wrong?"

She whirled on him. "Momma cooked breakfast."

Jerry wasn't sure what to say. "You're not happy she cooked? She didn't have to. I'm sure Fred has someone who can do that."

"Of course he does. Fred has people to do everything. But that's not the point. Momma cooked breakfast because she was trying to impress you."

"Aww, that's nice."

Max glared at him. "No, it's not nice. She likes you. Only she shouldn't because you already have a girlfriend."

He was right that Max had picked up on the email. Or at least on his reaction to the email. "Holly is not my girlfriend."

"Then what is she?"

I don't know. "A woman I rescued from a wreck."

"You said you would never lie to me."

Jerry held up his hands. "I'm not lying, Max. Holly isn't my girlfriend."

"You want her to be."

Jerry blew out a sigh. "There was a time I did."

"And now?"

I don't know. Before he could voice the words out loud, Max turned and raced down the stairs while Jerry followed at a much slower pace.

April was standing in the middle of the enormous kitchen, her eyes shining as bright as the smile that graced her lips. On the island in front of her were golden-brown biscuits, scrambled eggs, and bacon. "I'm sorry I had Max wake you, but I didn't want your breakfast to get cold."

"She didn't wake me. I was just about to come

down." Max now sat in the sun-filled breakfast room with her feet pulled up in the chair in front of her. She met his gaze briefly, then returned to the breakfast sandwich she was working on. Jerry reverted his attention to April. "You didn't have to cook. I'm sure there is a staff for that. If not, there are plenty of restaurants in the area."

April handed him a plate. "Are you kidding? This is my dream kitchen. It's well-stocked and even has a gas stove. Oh, how I miss cooking with gas."

Jerry scooped some eggs onto his plate and added several pieces of bacon. "If there is gas in your town, you should be able to run a gas line to your house."

"There is already gas in the house. I just need someone to put a line in the kitchen. It was in the works until I fired the handyman." April shrugged as she loaded her plate. "I'm looking for someone new, but everyone is all booked up at the moment."

Jerry started to offer his services and stopped when he felt Max staring at him. "It shouldn't be a big job if you find someone to do it."

April took her plate to the breakfast room and sat next to Max. "Oh, what I wouldn't give to have a room like this. Especially in the dead of winter. Wouldn't that be nice, Max? We could eat our breakfast and watch it snow."

It was easy to see why the room had captivated her so. An offshoot of the kitchen, the room was rounded and consisted mostly of large windows that looked out over the pool. Even the ceiling was mostly glass. A double-sided gas fireplace was on the far end of the room closest to the kitchen. Sitting here with April and Max, it was easy to get caught up in the illusion of a happy little family, or it would have been if Max didn't scowl at him every time he looked at her. Jerry picked up the biscuit, took a bite, then held it up, admiring it. "Homemade?"

April nodded as she took a bite of egg.

Jerry smiled. "They remind me of home. My granny used to make homemade biscuits. She would spend hours standing over the stove every Sunday. She'd fix fried chicken, pork chops or maybe a big roast turkey with all the trimmings, but there were always biscuits. Soft, flaky with golden-brown tops, just like these."

"Where's home?" April asked between bites.

"I grew up in Tennessee and spent a lot of time with my grandmother."

A frown creased April's brow. "Your parents weren't alive?"

"They lived right up the street. It's a long story, but my dad and I never really got along when I was young. Turns out it may have been a bit of a misunderstanding more than anything." Jerry looked directly at Max when he said the last part. "I think we mended fences when I was in Tennessee a few months back. I'm not sure that was a good thing because now my parents think I need to go visit them for Thanksgiving."

"You should consider yourself lucky they want you around. Some families are so messed up, they couldn't care less." April blushed and lowered her eyes.

Max stood and gathered her plate. "You're lucky you had a grandmother that wanted you around. Mom's family don't care about either of us."

Granny would have loved you. Not sure how to respond, Jerry looked to April for help.

"She's okay. Maxine is a tough kid," April whispered.

"My name's Max," she called out from the kitchen area.

"It's not nice to eavesdrop, Maxine."

"I can't help it if I have good ears." Max grinned.

Jerry's phone chimed. Max's smile faded as he reached for it. Jerry purposely held the phone where April could see it. "It's a message from Fred letting me know he picked up Savannah from the airport. They are on their way back, and he wants to know if anyone needs anything."

April shook her head. "Nothing he can pick out."

Jerry looked at her over his cell phone. "But there is something?"

April's blush deepened. "That swimming pool out back looks rather inviting. We were in such a hurry to come find you that I didn't think to bring swimsuits. Max has been swimming in shorts. It never dawned on me to think we would need one."

Her comment reminded him that he was the reason she was there. She'd cared enough to drop everything and set out in search of him. "Don't worry. If Savannah is here, there will be shopping involved. I'm sure she would love some company."

Max's face brightened. "Can I go too?"

Jerry returned his phone to his pocket. "I'm sure she wouldn't mind."

"Are you coming shopping with us?" Max asked, returning to her chair.

"And just what's so funny about me going shopping?" Jerry asked when April giggled.

April's giggles continued. "Because men don't shop."

"If you ladies will excuse me for a moment, I have a point to make." Jerry pushed back from his chair, glad he'd thought to put his keys in his pocket. Gunter followed him to his Durango, where Jerry retrieved two bags. Returning to the house, he peeked inside before setting them in front of Max and April.

Max immediately dug into her bag, pulling out the puzzles he'd bought for her in Mystic. "You bought these for me?"

Jerry nodded, pleased to see the smile had returned to her face. "I did." He looked at April, who'd yet to open her bag. "Aren't you going to open it?"

"Yeah, Mom, open it," Max urged.

April peered inside the bag, and her eyes grew wide. She pulled the box from the bag, carefully opening it. She pulled it out, turning it from side to side. "Jerry, how on earth did you know I collect teapots? Look, Max, it has ladybugs on it."

The truth of the matter was he hadn't known. But the instant he saw the two-sectioned yellow teapot cup combo with red ladybugs, he knew he had to buy it. Now seeing it in April's hands and the way her eyes sparkled when she studied it, he knew he'd given it to the right person.

April squinted her eyes at Max. "Are you sure you didn't tell him I collect teapots?"

Max crossed her heart with her finger. "Nope."

"I stand corrected. I guess some men do shop. Thank you, Jerry. I'm not sure what possessed you to buy it for me, but it is perfect." April returned the pot to the box with trembling hands. "I'll be right back."

"Where's she going?" Jerry asked when April hurried from the room.

"To cry," Max replied sourly. "After she left Randy, she made a promise that she wouldn't ever let another man see her cry."

Jerry ached to go after her, but he wasn't good with crying. He looked at Max. "Maybe you should go check on her."

Max remained seated. "She'll be okay. Just don't mention the crying when she comes back. You didn't really buy it for Mom, did you?"

"Yes, I did. I just didn't know it at the time." He looked directly at her so she could see the truth in his words. "Max, I know you are protective over your mom. I promise you I am not trying to hurt her. I care about you and your mother very much."

"It's not enough." Max pushed from her chair, scraping it across the tile floor. "We don't want you to care about us, Jerry. We want you to love us."

Jerry watched as Max ran off in the same direction as her mother had gone only a few moments earlier.

Gunter ran after her, then hesitated, looking back at Jerry as if to say, *You idiot, go after them*. When Jerry stayed rooted, Gunter followed Max up the stairs. A moment later, he heard a door slam in the distance.

Jerry stood and began gathering the breakfast dishes. He might not be good at showing his feelings, but dishes he could do.

Chapter Six

For the second time in as many days, Jerry watched April and Max get into a vehicle and drive away from him. His consolation: this time, the separation was temporary, as they were on their way to the mall to do some shopping with Savannah. Barney and a bodyguard who doubled as a driver went along to accompany them and double as security. Though none of their lives were in danger, Jerry felt better knowing the men were with them both to help maneuver them through town and as another set of eyes to keep them safe, since Gunter was staying with him.

Fred came up beside him. "We might not see them for a while."

Jerry chuckled. "What did April say when you handed her the credit card?"

"She balked at first. Then I reminded her Max was on the job and told her it was one of the perks." Fred turned to him. "Why didn't you just tell her you were footing the bill and to shop to her heart's content?"

Because I don't want to complicate things even

more than they already are. Jerry shrugged off the thought. "Because if she knew I was paying the bill, I think April would be more frugal with her purchases."

"I let her know there was no limit. It's probably going to cost you. Should I tell the driver to let me know if they try to test the lack of limit at a car lot?"

Jerry smiled and shook his head. "I don't think that's necessary."

"Okay, it's your dough. Although I still think it would be easier to just marry the woman."

Jerry let the comment slide. "Gunter and I are going to take off for a bit. I have something I want to check out."

Fred looked past him. Jerry knew the man was searching for the dog. Not seeing him, Fred sighed. "You think you've got a lead on our guy?"

Jerry shrugged. "Not sure. I got a hit on something. If it turns out to be something important, I'll give you a call. If not, I'll drive around for a while and see if anything calls to me."

"Want me to come with you?"

Though Jerry knew the man wished to be included, he waved him off. He worked better when it was just him and Gunter. When others got involved, they wanted to chat to fill the silence. While good for most occasions, it was not when one was trying to channel things that preferred solitude. "I've got this, thanks. I promise to keep you posted."

"Okay, it's probably best I hang around here anyway. Susie is coming in today. I doubt she'll be happy to learn she missed the shopping trip."

Jerry shook his head. "There will be more shopping. This area has plenty of malls and stores to peruse. I doubt they can hit them all in one day."

Fred smiled. "It's a good thing we're paying you well."

Jerry remembered the look on April's face when she saw the teapot. It would be worth every penny to see her eyes sparkle like that again. "I'm going to take off. My first stop isn't too far from here. Keep your phone close in case I need you."

Jerry started to call to Gunter and saw the dog paying extra attention to an area halfway between the house and the gatehouse. Crouched into a bow, the K-9 sniffed at a seemingly innocuous spot in the yard. Jerry motioned toward Gunter. "The dog seems to have found something in the yard."

Fred looked in the direction he pointed. "Any doubt I had about there being a dog is gone."

"Why's that?"

Though they were the only two around, Fred lowered his voice. "Remember me telling you we have some very important guests?"

Jerry raised an eyebrow. "You buried them in the yard?"

Fred chuckled. "Not hardly. Let's just say there is more to the property than meets the eye."

"You mean bunkers?"

"Bunkers, communications, and other things that are on a need-to-know basis. When I say this is a safe house, I mean it doesn't get much safer, except, of course, for other seemingly normal houses placed strategically within cities around the country. If it's a major city, we probably have a safe house or two somewhere nearby. We have some in rural settings as well."

Jerry looked Fred in the eye. "If you're telling me this now, what would you fill me in on if I was really read into the program?"

Fred waggled his brows. "Want to find out?"

Jerry shook his head. "I'm okay with my head in the sand for the time being."

Fred clapped him on the shoulder. "I'm wearing you down. I can tell."

Jerry whistled for Gunter.

Fred lifted his head, staring off into the distance. He sighed. "You know, McNeal, it's kind of like a kid looking for Santa Claus."

Jerry tilted his head. "What is?"

"You know he's real because there are presents under the tree each Christmas morning. But that doesn't keep you from trying your best to stay awake each Christmas Eve just to get a glimpse of him." Fred winked. "One of these days, I will see him for myself."

Jerry smiled. "The dog or the fat man?"

"Either one would make me a happy man. For now, I'll settle for a serial killer."

Jerry turned toward his Durango. "I can take a hint."

"McNeal?"

"Yeah, Fred?"

"Watch your six. We don't know what the man is capable of if he's cornered."

"Roger that," Jerry replied.

Gunter was waiting for him in the passenger seat when he got in. Jerry crept down the long driveway, looking to see if he could see anything out of place near the spot the dog had keyed on. *Not even a seam in the grass.* Jerry wondered if there was a hatch or if whoever was down there came and went via the guard shack. While he was admittedly curious, that curiosity wasn't enough to entice him to sign on for the full details. Besides, he already knew more than he should. He had a feeling if he waited him out long enough, Fred would eventually tell him everything he wished to know.

Jerry took a right out of the subdivision, then turned left onto Hanbury, following it the short distance to 168 North. As soon as he was on 168, his neck began to tingle, and as he passed the Mt. Pleasant exit, it had increased to a full crawl.

Gunter barked an excited bark and disappeared.

Jerry saw the sign for exit 12 and thought that was where he was headed. He knew he was mistaken when Gunter reappeared wearing his K-9 police vest just as Jerry noticed the man in the leather jacket and motorcycle helmet sitting on the guardrail at the base of the overpass. Gunter lifted his head and growled.

Jerry looked to see several buzzards soaring overhead. *Crap.* He slowed and turned on his emergency flashers as he made his way to the side of the road, inching over as close to the ditch as he dared. He pressed the button for the Uconnect. "Call Fred."

Fred answered almost immediately. "That was fast. Does this mean we can all go home?"

As if it is ever that easy. "No, more like time to go to work."

"What do you have?"

Jerry looked at the guardrail, which was now empty. "A dead body."

"Another redhead?"

"No. Just a guy who never made it home." Jerry had hoped it was just a spirit who was haunting the spot where he died, but he knew that wasn't the whole of it. Both the pull and the buzzards told him they would find a body among the forest of trees that sat to the right of the guardrail. "Get on 168 North. I'm at the base of the overpass just before Kempsville Road. And, Fred?"

"Yeah, Jerry?"

"Bring friends." Jerry hung up, waited for traffic

to clear and walked to the front of the Durango. He crossed one leg in front of the other as he leaned against the grill. He whistled to get Gunter's attention. Still wearing his vest, the K-9 ran up from the woods and looked at him expectantly. "Go get your buddy. I need to talk to him before the crew arrives."

Gunter barked, did an excited circle, then raced back into the woods. He returned a few moments later with the spirit. The guy was wearing the same leather jacket, only this time, he carried the helmet under his right arm.

The spirit looked at Gunter. "Cool dog. You know he's dead, right?"

It's easy to forget most of the time. Jerry nodded. "What's your name, buddy?"

"Roy. Roy Rodgers."

Jerry raised an eyebrow.

The spirit wiped at his helmet. "Hey, no wisecracks. I had to listen to enough of them while I was alive."

Jerry lost the smile. "Okay, Mr. Rodgers, care to tell me what happened?"

Roy sighed. "Nothing much to tell. I got off work at Wawa and never made it home."

Jerry looked toward the guardrail. "Did you fall asleep at the wheel?"

"The exact opposite. I was hyped up on coffee and felt the need for speed." Roy grinned. "I was skimming through the tube and caught a couple minutes of *Top Gun* while getting dressed for work that evening. I've driven this road more times than I can count. Rarely have I done the speed limit. Traffic was bunched up about a mile back, and I left them in the dust. I mean, I was really flying. I'm not sure what happened. I think I might have hit a rock or something. One minute, I was hunkered down enjoying the ride, and then I was speeding through the trees. Next thing I knew, I was in the middle of the interstate waving my hands for someone to stop. There was this truck, and he was coming straight for me. I was like, oh, this is going to hurt, but it didn't. I was like, cool. Then I was like, oh, so not cool. I was always scared of dying, but when it happened, it was just over."

"Do you know when it happened?"

"A week. Two weeks. I don't know. I've just been sitting on the guardrail trying to figure out what I'm supposed to do next. I thought maybe there'd be a light. I mean, you always hear about them, but the only lights I've seen are the headlights from all these cars. I was okay watching traffic until the birds showed up. You're lucky you saw me. Another few minutes and the birds would have landed, and I would have been back down by the bike. As long as I'm down there, they stay away. I know I'm dead and all, so I don't need that body, but they're buzzards, and well, that just ain't right. So, what are you, like a ghost whisperer or something?"

Jerry nodded. "Something like that."

"Cool. I thought that stuff only happened on television. So, what happens to me now?"

"My friends should be here any moment. They will find your remains and contact your family to let them know what happened. I'm sure they are worried."

"Yeah, okay. But what happens to me? I mean, I seem to be stuck here."

Jerry rolled his neck. "I can't make any promises, but I think once things are cleaned up, you'll be able to move around."

"Around where?" Roy pressed.

The heck if I know. Jerry shrugged. "Wherever you want."

"What about the white light?"

Jerry hated this part. He shrugged. "Buddy, this gift didn't come with an instruction manual. I'm just telling you what I know. The rest you're going to have to figure out on your own."

Gunter barked.

Jerry looked to see Fred's town car pull in behind his SUV.

"Where's your DB?" Fred asked when he joined them.

"Who's the suit, and what's a DB?" Roy asked.

"His name's Fred." Jerry pointed toward the guardrail. "Down there. His name's Roy Rodgers."

Fred chuckled. "Poor man. Probably got his butt kicked in school over that one. What kind of mom does that to a kid?"

"Hey, leave my mom out of this." Roy's energy intensified. "Tell him to leave my momma out of this."

Jerry looked at Fred. "You just insulted his mother."

Fred's eyes grew wide. "You mean he's here?"

Jerry shook his head. "That's how I found him."

"He owes my mom an apology."

Jerry rolled his neck. "He didn't mean anything by it."

Fred wrinkled his brow. "What'd I miss?"

"You insulted his mother."

"I did what?"

Jerry sighed. "Just say you're sorry."

"Tell him to say it like he means it," Roy insisted.

Jerry looked Fred in the eye. "Give the man a sincere apology."

"I'm sorry, Mr. Rodgers. I didn't mean to insult you or your mother. I'm sure you had a splendid childhood."

"Tell him to get down on his knees and beg my forgiveness."

Jerry resisted the urge to roll his eyes. "Not going to happen."

Fred leaned in a little closer. "What's not going to happen?"

Jerry held up his hand.

"What's stopping me from pushing him down myself?" Roy asked.

Gunter stepped in front of Fred. Ears back and hackles raised, he bared his teeth.

Roy faded in and out. "Call off your dog, man. I was only having a little fun."

Jerry motioned Gunter to stand down. The dog eased his stance but remained in front of Fred. Jerry firmed his chin. "Anything happens to this man, and I'll turn the dog loose."

Fred's face paled.

Roy held up his hands. "It's cool, man. I didn't mean any harm. Like I said, I was just having a little fun."

Jerry looked at the sky, which was now devoid of buzzards. "The birds are gone. Maybe you should wait by your body." Jerry blew out another sigh when Roy disappeared. He looked at Fred. "Boss, from this point on, I want you to assume we are not alone when we are talking about the deceased."

Fred lowered his voice. "Did you just threaten a ghost with a ghost?"

Jerry shrugged. "I was all out of silver bullets."

Chapter Seven

The wail of a siren sifted through the air. A few moments later, a black Mustang topped the hill. Unmarked, except for the police lights fitted into the grill, it moved to the left lane and slowed to pull onto the narrow strip of grass that separated the north and southbound lanes of Chesapeake 168. A Chesapeake police officer got out and made his way across traffic to where Jerry and Fred stood. "Officer Emory. I understand you may have found a body?"

Fred greeted the officer with his badge and ID. "Fred Jefferies; this here is Jerry McNeal. He's the one who discovered the body."

Actually, I haven't seen the body, but I've had quite the conversation with the spirit of the man who used to inhabit it, Jerry thought to himself.

The officer looked at him as if waiting for him to produce ID. "So, where's the body?" Officer Emory asked when Jerry didn't offer any.

Jerry pointed to the trees. "Through those trees."

Emory frowned. "How far?"

"No, clue, but by the speed the bike was going when it lost control, probably in a ways," Jerry replied.

"Speed? You mean you saw it happen? Why didn't you call for an ambulance?"

Jerry looked at the man. "No need for one. The man's been dead for a week or two."

Emory cocked an eyebrow.

Before he could ask any more questions, Fred intervened. "Mr. McNeal has a special talent. He heads up our psychic division."

A smile played at Emory's mouth. Jerry had to give him credit. At least he hadn't resorted to a full-fledged belly laugh. Jerry planted his feet, ready to argue his case if need be. "Listen, I know this sounds like a crock. I'm not sure I'd believe it if the shoe was on the other foot. But it's true. The man's name is Roy Rodgers. He looks to be in his early to mid-twenties. He said he worked at Wawa and disappeared a week or so ago."

"Wait, I've seen a flyer on a guy by that name. He went missing last week. You're saying you talked to the guy? A moment ago, you said he was dead."

"He is."

"And you had a conversation with him?"

Fred grinned like a proud papa. "I told you he is talented." Fred nodded toward the median. "White and his team are here."

Emory's face paled. "What the heck is the FBI doing here?"

Fred's grin turned into a chuckle. "He's talented. I'm connected."

Emory stared open-mouthed as Fred waded through the slow-moving, gawking traffic and joined several others, each of whom wore black windbreakers with FBI initials clearly visible. "Who the heck is that guy?" Emory asked, finding his voice.

"I'd tell you, but then I'd have to kill you." Jerry chuckled. "Sorry, I've always wanted an excuse to say that."

Emory blew out a disgusted sigh. "This isn't an FBI case. It's not even a case for whoever the heck he is. What is he even doing here?"

Jerry rocked back on his heels. "I called him."

Emory narrowed his eyes. "What, you've never heard of 911?"

"I assure you, the FBI being here has nothing to do with you or the Chesapeake Police Department. I am sure you all do a fine job. I called Fred because he's my boss. Fred shoots from the hip and is used to dealing with some heavy hitters. This won't fall back on you in any way. I know you're skeptical, but I spoke with Roy. He assured me this was all on him, that he was going too fast and there was no one close enough to have seen what happened. I told that to Fred, who will make sure to relay it."

Jerry understood the man's frustration, but he also knew enough to know that if Fred hadn't called in reinforcements, they would both be there for hours giving statements and telling everyone that showed up how it was that Jerry had just happened to find the body. As it was, Fred would tell the story to White, and he would see to the rest. Was it an FBI job? No. Did Fred care? Probably not. Fred didn't have any ill feelings toward the police, nor did he find them to be incompetent. Fred was a man who was used to getting things done. He was also adept at using the resources at his disposal to accomplish what was needed. If that meant bringing the FBI in to oversee an investigation on an ill-fated motorcycle crash, then so be it. Jerry pulled out his wallet and handed officer Emory one of his cards. "If this blows up on you, give me a call."

Emory pocketed the card. "Thanks. Yeah, it does sound a bit far out there, but no more than some of the crap I've seen on TikTok."

Jerry suddenly regretted giving the guy his card. He lowered his voice. "This doesn't go on TikTok."

Emory shook his head. "Of course not."

Jerry didn't believe him. "My name comes up on TikTok, and the FBI will be the least of your troubles. Got it?"

"Wait, are you threatening a police officer?"

Jerry looked directly into the officer's body camera. "Only if that police officer were to be stupid enough to put my name or anything about what I do on social media."

A dispatcher's voice called out over Emory's police radio, asking him his status. Emory sighed and keyed the mike. "Good status. I'm going to send you a name." Emory pulled out his cell phone and typed in Roy's name, followed by the word "deceased." He looked at Jerry. "Don't want to put it on the radio. Too many ears on the scanner."

It didn't slip past Jerry that the man had acted without confirming the news. *He believes me. Hopefully, that trust includes my stance on social media recognition.* Jerry nodded his understanding.

Fred and the others started in their direction. When they approached, Fred jerked a thumb toward Jerry. "This is the guy I was telling you about. Jerry McNeal, Malcolm White."

Malcolm White was a tall African American man with intense eyes. His dark, ringless hand nearly swallowed Jerry's as he reached to shake it. White released his grip and smiled a sly smile. "Your reputation precedes you, Mr. McNeal. Fred here has told me what you are capable of, but I didn't think I would be privy to witnessing it myself. According to my contacts at the Chesapeake Police Department, this Rodgers guy has been missing for just over a week. You've been in town less than twenty-four hours and already solved one missing person's case. If you ever get tired of working for this guy, give me a call. We could use someone with your talents in our neck of the woods."

Jerry resisted looking at Emory. The man was already unhappy about the FBI showing up. Having them show up with vital information would cut even deeper. "I'm good, for now."

White sighed. "I knew you were going to say that. Either way, Fred and I had a discussion about some things we'd like your help with."

Jerry frowned. Before he could reply, Fred spoke up.

"Traffic is backing up in both directions. We'd better get out of your hair so you guys can get this cleaned up."

"You can't leave yet," Officer Emory called as Fred and Jerry moved toward their vehicles.

Jerry turned and saw White step in front of Emory. "What do you say we go see if we can find that body of yours."

Fred pivoted toward Jerry. "Meet me back at the house."

Jerry nodded and looked for Gunter, who'd disappeared at the same time Roy did. Jerry wasn't sure if the dog was keeping an eye on the spirit or helping him fend off the birds. Not that it mattered, as he knew Gunter would find him when he was finished. He got inside the Durango and started it up. One of the men who'd arrived with White held up a hand and stepped into oncoming traffic, which had dwindled to a crawl. Jerry eased into the lane, and Fred pulled out behind him, following as he led the way to the Kempsville exit, made a loop, and got back on the highway heading south.

Traffic backed up over the overpass. Jerry heard a siren and looked to see blue lights behind him, blinking his surprise when he realized they were attached to the grill of Fred's town car. *Showoff. Times like this, I really miss my cruiser.*

Fred eased to the shoulder and motioned for Jerry to follow as he made his way up the emergency lane. As soon as they passed the accident scene, traffic opened up, allowing them to smooth back into the lane.

As Jerry rounded the Hanbury exit, Gunter joined him in the SUV. Jerry smiled at his furry friend, glad to see he was no longer wearing his police vest. "Thanks for having our six back there, dog."

Gunter smiled a K-9 smile.

It didn't take long to get back to the house. Fred was just getting out of his car when Jerry parked. Jerry slid out of the driver's seat and met him. Gunter sat and scratched at an imaginary itch. "I should have let Roy beat the crap out of you."

Gunter stopped scratching and looked at Fred.

Fred cocked an eyebrow. "What's got you so riled?"

"As if you don't know," Jerry huffed. "What was that crap back there? You're not my pimp, so stop acting like it."

Fred's lip twitched. "I assure you I am no one's pimp. If you're talking about what White said, he told me about a situation they are watching. I didn't commit you to anything. I told him I would run it past you. He knows why we are in the area and has offered any assistance we need. He was hoping to get the same professional courtesy. I've told you time and again I will not dictate what you are to do. When are you going to trust me?"

Jerry felt his anger ebb. He did trust Fred. At least, he wanted to. Mostly, he was upset that Fred was talking about his abilities to total strangers. "It's just that I've spent most of my life flying under the radar. The last thing I want is for my life to become a circus. I just threatened a cop. How's that for a fine how do you do? Someone would have talked to me like that, and I would have stuck my nightstick up his…"

Fred cut him off. "Threatened a cop, how?"

"The guy mentioned TikTok. I warned him about putting my name on social media."

Fred's jaw relaxed. "Don't worry about social media. We have someone monitoring that. We see something we don't like, we take it down."

Feeling Jerry's tension ease, Gunter went back to scratching his itch. Jerry scratched his own head and looked at the dog. "You'd better not have picked up any fleas in those woods."

Fred peered from side to side. "I assume you are

talking to the dog. Can ghost dogs get fleas, or are they ghost fleas?"

Jerry sighed. "I don't have a clue. I only know he's scratching."

"He hasn't scratched before?"

Now that Fred mentioned it, Gunter had scratched many times. "Maybe it's a phantom scratch."

Fred frowned. "Excuse me?"

"I have a friend who had his leg amputated. He told me even though the leg is gone, he still feels it. Sometimes it hurts, and sometimes it itches just like it is still there."

Fred nodded. "Phantom pain. I've heard of it."

"Maybe that's what's going on with the dog."

"Or, maybe he has dry skin. I once had a dog with eczema," Fred offered.

Gunter stopped scratching, and they both stared at Fred. Jerry chuckled. "You know he's a ghost, right? He doesn't actually have any skin." Jerry decided to change the subject when Gunter lowered to the ground and placed his muzzle on his front paws. "Emory was a bit put off you brought in the FBI. I told him not to take it personally."

Fred smiled. "So, what you're saying is the kid thinks I am an overbearing pain in the keister?"

Jerry matched his smile. "Something like that."

Fred's smile turned into a chuckle. "I recall a time not too long ago when you thought the same thing."

"Who said I still don't?" Jerry winked. "I told him you were a man used to getting things done."

"Speaking of which, I would like you to take a drive with me."

"Where to?"

"I told White we would meet with his man. Now don't look at me like that. It's just a quick meeting, and we're only there to listen. How involved we get is strictly up to you. *Comprende*?"

Jerry glanced at Gunter. When the dog didn't seem to object, he nodded. "Understood."

"Good. We're supposed to meet him in fifteen minutes. I'll text to let him know we are on our way. While I'm at it, I'm going to text Barney to let them know to take the back roads if they are returning anytime soon. I have a feeling 168 is going to be bumper to bumper the rest of the day."

"That was pretty cool how we were able to cut around traffic like that."

Fred tilted his head. "What, the lights? They're called police lights. All the cool kids have them. Why? Do you want some?"

Yes, yes I do. Jerry worked to contain his excitement. "I could be talked into it."

"McNeal, there are times when your face is hard to read. This is not one of those times. Let's get things cleaned up here, and we'll get you set up with our guys." Fred clamped him on the shoulder. "Let's take my car. If you behave yourself, I might even authorize you a siren."

Chapter Eight

Jerry lowered the back of his chair, only to raise it again a second later. He shifted in his seat, worming around trying to find a comfortable position, then reached for the window button.

Fred beat him to it, locking the window to prevent it from lowering. "What is wrong with you? I have the urge to tell you to sit on your hands. I swear, you fidget worse than a toddler."

"Sorry, I can't get comfortable. I'm used to driving. It feels weird sitting on this side. Normally, Gunter sits in the passenger seat." *Unless Granny shows up.* Jerry felt inclined to leave that part out.

"Ribs still bothering you?"

Jerry nodded.

"So, where is the dog now?"

Jerry jerked his thumb toward the backseat. "Looking over your right shoulder."

Fred looked in the rearview mirror and sighed. "Someday," he mumbled as he took exit 8A to Hillcrest Parkway and continued to the far rear of the Target parking lot. He'd no sooner backed into a parking space than a black SUV pulled alongside them. Fred unlocked the window and pushed the button to lower it. Jerry smiled as Gunter stuck his head through the glass behind him.

The driver of the SUV powered down his window. "Jefferies?"

Fred nodded. "That'd be me."

"I'm Kyle Struthers. White sent me."

"I figured it was either that or you were about to offer me a drug deal. Glad it wasn't the latter. I don't feel like arresting anyone today. Come on over. It will be easier than talking through the window." Fred turned to Jerry. "The dog's not going to bite him, is he?"

"Hasn't bitten anyone that hasn't deserved it." Jerry recalled the time Gunter bit him and rubbed at his arm.

Fred's eyes grew wide. "He bit you?"

Jerry nodded. "It was the first body we found. We were in the cemetery, and Gunter started digging up a grave. I thought he was being destructive. I tried to stop him, and he bit me. It wasn't his fault. I didn't know he was working. Turns out, he was only trying to show me where the body was."

"Patti? She was your first, right?" Fred asked.

Jerry sighed at the mention of his high school friend. *Patti was the first of many things. First kiss. First real girlfriend. First heartbreak.* First person he cared about to have died at the hands of a serial killer, yet here he was doing nothing to find her killer. Jerry swallowed. "Yes, she was the first."

Struthers tried the back door handle and knocked on the window.

Jerry composed himself. "Better let the guy in before he thinks you're messing with him."

"Maybe it would be better if you sit in the back," Fred suggested.

"I'm not moving to the back. The guy's FBI. If I were in his shoes, I would think that to mean you don't trust me. Now open the door."

Fred sighed and hit the button.

Struthers opened the door and laughed a nervous laugh. "For a moment, I half expected you to drive off. Everything okay in here?"

"Just fine," Fred answered without giving any explanation.

Gunter backed away from the door enough to allow Struthers into the car. Struthers tried to move to the center of the seat, then stopped. While neither Fred nor Struthers saw the reason, Jerry knew it was because Gunter refused to give up any more space. Jerry motioned the dog over, ending the gesture by rubbing his hand over his head.

Struthers looked at Jerry and wrinkled his brow. "I didn't get your name. Are you two sure everything is okay, and there's not some kind of carbon monoxide leak or something?"

Jerry offered the man his hand. "McNeal. No need to call the men with the white coats. We've been having a bit of trouble with that back lock."

Fred turned in his seat and took charge of the conversation. "White said you guys have a situation you could use our help with. Said you'd brief us."

Struthers nodded. "Actually, we are just coming on board. This gang has been moving up the east coast, hitting places close to the state lines. If they run into trouble, they hop back over the state line. That's why we were called in."

"Who are they?" Fred asked.

Gunter leaned forward, sniffing at Struthers' ear. Struthers batted away the invisible assault. "No clue just yet. Nobody we've had our eyes on. They are pretty organized, though. When they hit, they hit hard. Kind of like a smash and grab, hitting several key places at once, then just disappear."

Jerry interrupted him. "What do you mean disappear?"

"Just that. It's like these guys are ghosts or something."

Fred looked at Jerry.

Jerry shook his head. "They prefer to be called spirits, and spirits don't steal things."

"What about poltergeists?" Struthers argued.

Jerry sighed. "Same thing."

"What?" Fred and Struthers asked at the same time.

"Spirits, ghosts, and poltergeists are all one and the same, and they don't steal. They borrow. They do it out of frustration because they can't communicate. Or for attention. On occasion, they do it because they were real jerks when they were alive, but they don't work in teams."

"What are you saying?"

Gunter, still messing with the man, now nosed at Struthers' crotch.

"Leave it!" Jerry realized he'd corrected the dog aloud and covered himself. "Sorry, I didn't mean to yell, but you need to leave it alone. Your guys are crooks, plain and simple."

Struthers looked as if he was ready to bolt from the car. It didn't help that Gunter was now licking the back of Struthers' hand. To Struthers, it would feel more like a cold sensation. Struthers pulled his hand back, rubbing the back of it with the fingers of the other. "So the disappearance is just a fluke?"

Jerry nodded. "If the guys are smart enough to avoid being captured for so long, they are smart enough to plot their heists in advance. A team this organized would not chance simply driving over the state line on a whim to see what kind of chaos they can cause. Now that I know what's going on, let me see what kind of feeling I get, and I'll let you know what I come up with."

"You mean if you come up with something?" Struthers corrected.

"No, I mean when. Now that you've made me aware, it will come." Jerry didn't want to tell the man he was already getting a tingle.

Gunter nosed at Struthers' head, and the man's hand went to the spot to scratch the phantom itch. "I thought you just dealt with ghosts."

Jerry shrugged. "Sometimes, I moonlight as a psychic detective."

Struthers looked at Fred. "So, what do I tell White?"

Fred pressed the button to unlock the door. "Tell him when we have something for him, we'll give him a call."

Struthers slid across the seat and got out. The look of relief on the man's face was instantaneous. He leaned his upper torso into the car while holding firmly to the door frame. "You know, I've heard you guys are an unconventional bunch, but brothers, that's putting it mildly." Before Struthers had a chance to close the door, Gunter leaned forward and licked the length of his face. Struthers gave a shudder, slammed the car door, and all but ran to his SUV.

Fred shook his head as he pushed the button to raise his window. "I might suggest White order a psych exam on that guy."

"No need."

"You didn't think he was acting a bit off?"

"You'd ask the same if you were being punked by the ghost of a ninety-pound police dog. Gunter was all over him, licking him and getting up in his grill." Jerry turned and faced Gunter. "You were a bad boy." Jerry sighed when Gunter raised his lip to show a K-9 smile and thumped his tail triumphantly against the back seat.

"Wait, you're telling me Struthers knew he was there?"

Jerry shook his head. "No, if he did, he would have said something. No, he probably felt like his skin was crawling or heaviness in the air. If either of us had so much as scratched, the man would have probably accused us of having bedbugs. He tried to move to the center, and Gunter refused to move. That one probably freaked him out a little."

"Aha!" Fred slapped his leg. "That's what Barney felt."

"Excuse me?"

"In the hotel bar. Barney tried to sit next to you and said it was as if he'd encountered an invisible wall. Gunter was sitting in the seat next to you, wasn't he?"

Jerry smiled. "He usually is."

"Crap."

"What?"

"That means I owe Barney an apology." Fred started the car, drove a couple of feet, and started to make a right onto Carmichael Way.

Jerry stopped him. "Take a left."

Fred did so without question, then made a right onto Edinburgh Parkway when Jerry pointed. They turned right into Edinburgh Meadows, a growing housing development with houses that would sell in the high seven figures. Fred looked over at Jerry. "Playing a hunch or house hunting?"

"Neither."

"Meaning?"

"My feelings aren't hunches."

"So, this is the place?"

"According to the hairs on the back of my neck, yes."

"What do we tell White?"

Jerry emitted another sigh. "Nothing yet."

"Why not?"

"Because it's too early."

"Quit thinking like a cop."

"What's that supposed to mean?"

"You're used to waiting until something goes down to make your move. Look at the bigger picture. We can be there waiting for them when they arrive."

"What if I don't know when they will arrive?"

"That's what the team is for, Jerry. You may be the divining rod that brings us here, but we will work together to catch these guys." Fred continued to speak as he drove through the well-to-do neighborhood. "That's what I've been trying to get through to you. You are now a part of our family and we look out for each other. It's the same with the Hash Mark Killer. You don't have to find him on your own. You got us this far. If you allow us to use our resources to help, we can nail this guy sooner."

Jerry wanted to agree. While he wanted to find this guy, he'd already wasted so much time homing in on other cases. "I don't like putting Susie in danger."

"We will have eyes on Susie at all times. She doesn't even have to get close to the killer other than to identify him, and that will only be a formality."

Jerry slid a glance toward Fred. "How so?"

"Because as soon as we have the SOB, we can do a DNA match to what we got from Rita's ring. Before you ask, he didn't show up on any of our databases."

"I still don't like using Susie as bait."

"You're forgetting, the sooner we catch this guy, the safer she'll be. The safer they'll all be. Let's get him before he kills anyone else." Fred cleared his voice. "Speaking of victims, I got word that Fiona's family finally let her go."

Jerry closed his eyes, picturing the redhead he'd last seen lying in a coma at Bethesda. *Fred's right. I can't do this alone. If not for Max, Fiona would probably have spent years lying in bed unable to move, speak, or even breathe on her own. Max is part of the family.* Gunter moved forward and placed his muzzle on Jerry's left shoulder. *Yes, boy, you are family too.* Jerry reached his hand to the dog, who sighed under his touch. "Okay."

"Okay, what?"

"All of it." Jerry spread his arms toward the houses. "Whatever is going on here, letting Susie come into the fold, all of it. I'm ready to concede that I need help."

"You say that as if you are admitting to an addiction."

Jerry shrugged. "Maybe in some way it is. There was a time I thought of this as my curse. But my family – my real family – showed me that it is a gift. Even my granny told me that I needed to let others help me. That's why she sent Gunter to be with me." Jerry looked over at Fred. "My granny's dead."

"I gathered that," Fred replied softly. "You and she were close?"

Jerry nodded. "Very."

"I'm sorry."

"Don't be. That's the best part of this gift. I still get to see her from time to time."

"Boy, McNeal, it must be something being you."

"It's something alright." Jerry reached up and scratched the dog once more. Gunter rewarded him with a K-9 kiss behind the ear.

Fred's phone chimed, and he checked the message. "Susie's almost to the house. How about you and I go say hello to our star witness? Unless, that is, you think there's more to see here."

Jerry looked over the neighborhood, studying the

impressive multilevel brick homes, which took up most of the lot they were sitting on. It wouldn't be too much longer, but whatever was going to happen wouldn't be today. He shook his head. "No, we're good for now."

Chapter Nine

Susie and her driver were just getting out of the SUV when they arrived. The driver went to the back, pulled out several suitcases, and headed for the door.

Susie's hair had reverted to its natural red color. Though not heavy to begin with, she was leaner than when he'd last seen her and her arms were well-toned, presumably from the kickboxing classes of which Fred spoke. She saw Jerry and smiled a warm smile. "You're a sight for sore eyes."

Fred moved up beside them. "How was the flight?"

Susie laughed a hearty laugh. "You're kidding, right?"

Fred glanced at Jerry. "I didn't think I was."

She laughed once more. "Dude, I flew here in a Learjet. How do you think it was? Then I get here and find I'm staying in a mansion. Pretty freaking incredible, that's how. What's with the dog? It looks like he's found a dead body. Maybe we should check. I'll show you how to do an autopsy."

Jerry turned to see Gunter sniffing at the same spot he'd keyed on earlier. *An underground communications system the likes of which you've never seen.* Knowing Fred wouldn't be happy if he divulged that information, Jerry made something up. "Probably smelling the deer that was in the yard earlier."

Fred looked to where they were staring and sighed. "Someday."

"What's with him?" Susie asked when Fred started toward the house.

Jerry lowered his voice. "He still hasn't seen him yet."

"The dog?"

"Yep."

"Bummer."

Jerry motioned her toward the house. "Did they tell you why you're here?"

"Sure. They said I deserved a holiday at the beach."

Jerry stopped in his tracks.

Susie laughed until she snorted. "Geez, Jerry, lighten up. I was kidding. You can't blame me for wanting to have a bit of fun. I jumped for joy when Fred asked if I was interested in helping catch that freak. I'd do just about anything to get out of house arrest."

"They don't allow you out of the house?"

"Sure they do, but not without my mommy. I mean, the lady's nice and all, but it's kind of a drag when people think you're bringing your mom everywhere."

"How old is the woman?"

"I don't know. Maybe a little older than you."

Jerry raised an eyebrow.

Susie laughed once more. "Seriously, dude. Lighten up. When was the last time you laughed?"

"I laugh all the time."

"No, I mean really laugh." She pointed to his stomach. "Come on, give me a chuckle, Jerry. Think Santa Claus. Let it start in your belly and work its way up."

"I don't chuckle."

"See, that's your problem. You need to unwind. When was the last time you were on a date?"

Jerry narrowed his eyes. "Have you been talking to my grandmother?"

She smiled. "No, just Savannah. She said you're hung up on some Holly chick, and since I was coming to Virginia that maybe I could take your mind off of her."

"Great."

"Great, what? You want to go out?"

"No. Great, Savannah has been hanging out with Max and April all day."

"What do Max and April have to do with anything?"

Before Jerry could answer, an SUV pulled into the driveway. Gunter barked and followed it up the drive wagging his tail. *April and Max are back.*

"You might not be Santa, but you just lit up like a Christmas tree." She craned her neck. "Who's in there that's got you all worked up?"

"I'm not worked up. I'm just happy to see they made it back without any trouble." Jerry worked to keep the smile off his face as the doors to the SUV opened, and everyone piled out. He ached to go greet them and ask how their shopping trip went, but knew Susie was watching him, so he remained in place.

April was the first to reach him. Her hands were full of bags, and even though she looked totally exhausted, she managed a smile. She looked Susie up and down, and her brow creased.

Jerry reached for her bags. "Here, let me help with those."

"It's alright. I can manage. I'm used to carrying my own bags."

Jerry opened the door, and April went inside without another word.

Way to go, McNeal.

Max came up the walk with Gunter all but prancing at her side.

"Looks like he missed you." Jerry smiled at Max. "Did you have fun shopping?"

"Yeah, it was cool," she replied without slowing down. Gunter followed her inside.

Susie tilted her head. "Ouch. Talk about the cold shoulder."

Susie was right. Something was wrong. "If you'll

excuse me, I would like to talk to Savannah alone."

"It's cool. I'm going to go check out my room."

Savannah looked up when he approached. "Ouch, what's eating you? Your aura's as dark as molasses."

Barney looked in his direction, then nudged the driver, who gathered the rest of the bags. Jerry watched as both men headed to the house. Jerry lowered his voice. "What's with April and Max?"

"What do you mean?"

"Don't give me that. Neither one of them said more than two words to me."

"I think they're upset with you."

Jerry struggled to keep his voice under control. "I can see that. What I want to know is why."

Savannah shrugged.

"Don't give me that. You've been with them all day."

"What do you think I am? A mind reader?"

"No, but you're a psychic and a darn good one. Now out with it."

"I didn't know April was hung up on you. Honest, I didn't."

"What did you do?"

"It was truly an accident. We were shopping, and April said something about Holly, and I asked her if she knew your girlfriend. I didn't know she was talking about Christmas decorations until I turned around and saw her pointing. Seriously, Jerry, I hadn't even seen the Christmas decorations before that. Why do they have them out now anyway? We still have to get through Halloween."

"What was said?"

"I didn't say much after that." She sighed. "Max kind of took it from there. She wanted to know what I knew about Holly, and then April wanted to know what Max knew. It turns out neither of us knew much, not that it mattered because, by then, the damage was done. April said she had a headache and wanted to come home. It kind of put a damper on things, but by then, we'd all pretty much gotten what we needed. Then Max had a meltdown when we were crossing the drawbridge."

Jerry's skin began to crawl at the mention of the drawbridge. "What drawbridge? What kind of meltdown?"

"I don't know the name of it. It wasn't like it was up or anything. She kept asking the driver to make sure the doors were locked."

"Did you feel anything?"

"Anything what?"

"A premonition or anything?"

Savannah shook her head. "I don't really get those. I can read a person, but I can't predict bad stuff if I don't want to. I've set boundaries and don't let bad stuff in. It's better for my aura if I don't accept negative energy. Now that you mention it, I guess it could have been a premonition. I thought she was just having a panic attack because it was a drawbridge. She seemed better after we got away from the bridge."

"Didn't I tell you to keep your wits about you? Our killer could be anywhere! How do you know you weren't within steps of him in the mall?" Jerry felt like grabbing her by the shoulders and shaking her, but it wouldn't do any good. Plus, he didn't want her to file an assault charge.

"I did have my guard up until we got into the car. The driver was driving, and Barney was with us. We were heading home, and, well, to be honest, Max and April's energy was bringing me down, so I cleared myself and said my protection mantras." Savannah started toward the door. "I'll go check on her."

Jerry sighed. "No, you go put your things away. I'll go check on her."

"Are you sure? She seems rather sore."

Jerry smiled a weak smile. "Yeah, I'm sure."

***

As Jerry walked up the stairs, he heard Max and April chatting. Though he couldn't hear what they were saying, their voices were light and filled with the laughter of a close mother-and-daughter bond. Jerry sighed, knowing that the moment they opened the door, a veil would come down, letting him know he was an outsider and no longer welcome in their world. Gunter shoved his head through the closed door, staring at him. He heard the unmistakable sound of Max's giggles and knew her to be laughing at the dog's antics.

Unwilling to intrude on their happiness, Jerry raised a finger to his lips, asking Gunter to keep his presence a secret. A large sitting area with a couch and several wingback chairs off the second floor hallway separated the bedrooms. He bypassed that and continued on to his room.

His grandmother appeared the second he entered the room. "Learn from your mistakes, Jerry. Don't let a silly misunderstanding keep you from finding happiness."

He instantly knew what mistake she was referring to. It had been the same with him and his dad and their constant turmoil when he was younger. If only his dad wouldn't have waited all those years to try and reach him. Maybe things would have been different between them.

"Don't put that all on your father. You need to shoulder some of the blame. I don't recall hearing how you went and told him your thoughts. Maybe if you had, it would have opened the door to communication."

Jerry studied her for a moment. "You know, I believe that is the first time I ever heard you take his side. Besides, you were my mentor. I don't remember you encouraging me to go talk to him and tell him what was on my mind."

"That's because I wanted you all to myself. I was a lonely old lady, and I enjoyed having my grandson around. Listen, if you want to remind me of my faults, we can go over those later. But for now, you need to make this right."

Jerry shook his head. "I'm pretty sure it's too late for that. It's a whole mixed-up affair of he said, she said. That's why I prefer working alone – things are much less complicated."

"And a lot lonelier. You can't run from matters of the heart, Jerry. They always catch up with you."

"How can you know what's in my heart when I don't know?"

"You don't know because you won't let your mind settle down long enough to listen to it. That Susie girl was right. The second you saw April and Max get out of the car, your face lit up. Have you even stopped to question why you haven't bothered to open the email from Holly?"

"I've been too busy." It was a lie, and he knew she knew it. The pathetic truth of the matter was he was afraid to read it. His feelings were jumbled up enough without adding to the turmoil.

Granny looked toward his computer. "You're not busy now."

"Now's not the time!" He instantly regretted yelling at her, but her meddling wasn't helping.

"Why not?"

"Because I have a killer to catch!"

"And yet here you are. Don't you think that means a part of you realizes how important Max and April are to you? Instead of going off and doing what you came to Virginia to do, you're up here trying to make things right."

Jerry looked around the room. "You see how far that's gotten me."

"Because you are afraid."

"I'm not afraid of them."

"No, you're afraid of yourself. Afraid of letting anyone in."

"I let Gunter in." *Not that I had a choice.*

"You did not. You were ready to give him back to Manning. The dog held his ground and wormed his way into your heart. Believe it or not, there is room in there for more. You just have to let them in."

"I don't know how. What if I screw it up like I've screwed everything else up in my life?"

Granny walked over and placed her hand alongside his cheek. Instantly, all the worry he felt was gone. "I failed you by keeping you all to myself for so long. I thought I was protecting you from the cruelness of the world, but in reality, I was keeping you from spreading your wings." She leaned in and kissed him on the forehead, and then she was gone.

Jerry felt Gunter lean against his leg. He turned and saw Max staring at him with unblinking eyes.

Chapter Ten

Max looked around the room as if expecting to see someone. "Gunter pushed the door open. Are you alright, Jerry? I thought I heard you yelling at someone."

"I'm fine, Max. I was just talking to my grandmother."

Her gaze scanned the room. "Did she leave on account of me?"

Jerry shook his head. "No, we were finished talking. As a matter of fact, I was just coming to find you. Savannah said you got upset. Something about the drawbridge. Was it a premonition?"

Max nodded. "Savannah didn't pick up on it. How come? I thought she was like us."

"Make sure you don't fall into the trap of thinking that just because someone is psychic, they know everything that's going to happen. If I had a dollar for every time someone asked me for the lottery numbers, I'd be rich."

"I thought you were rich."

"Let's go to the sitting area so we can talk." Jerry led the way and sat in one of the wingback chairs as

Max climbed onto the couch, tucking her feet under her bottom the way he'd seen April do so many times. Gunter jumped up beside her and lay with his head in her lap. Jerry heard a door click.

April stepped into the hall. "Am I intruding?"

"Not at all." Jerry stood and motioned toward a chair. "I'm afraid the couch is taken."

April tilted her head toward the couch. "Gunter?"

Jerry loved that April had become so accepting of things she couldn't see or feel in such a short time. "I think it's safe to assume he is attached to both of us." Jerry waited for April to sit, then eased back into his chair.

April's brow knitted as she watched him sit. "I like knowing she has a guardian angel."

Jerry looked at Max. "Me too. Savannah told me something happened on the drawbridge. I was just about to talk to Max about it."

April frowned. "Max wanted the doors locked, but I don't recall her making a fuss about it."

"I have a feeling it was a little more than wanting the doors locked. Am I right, Max?"

Max nodded.

"You had a premonition?" Jerry continued.

She nodded once more.

"Tell me about it."

"There were a bunch of guys, and they were hiding in the ditch. They waited until the drawbridge swung open, and there were cars waiting in line. Then the men came running out from both sides of the road. They all had something in their hands that let them break out windows. It was fast. They broke the windows, pointed guns, and robbed everyone."

"Is that all?"

"No, there was a black SUV blocking the cars, so they couldn't leave. When the men were done, they jumped into the SUV and left."

"These men, what kind of guns did they have?"

"Pistols mostly. But I remember a couple had shotguns. There was another guy – I think he was in charge."

"What makes you say that?"

"Because he didn't go to the car windows. He just stood back, watching with a shotgun in his hand. At least I think it was a shotgun. It looked kind of different. He's the one that told them when it was time to leave."

April leaned forward in her chair. "The drawbridge wasn't even open. You saw all that while we were driving over it?"

Max nodded.

Gunter raised his head.

Jerry looked to see Fred topping the stairs. He walked to where they were sitting and looked Jerry in the eye. "Susie is firing up the laptop we want her to use. I thought maybe April would like to help her figure out what to say."

April scrambled from her chair then paused, focusing on Max. "Are you okay, honey?"

"I'm good," Max assured her.

Jerry felt his jaw tighten but refrained from calling the man out in front of April. He kept his cool until she was out of sight. "I thought we were going to keep her out of this."

Fred blew out a sigh. "We were and still are to a point. She's already been poking around in the group. This way, she feels like she is involved without putting herself in danger."

"It's okay, Jerry," Max assured him. "Mr. Jefferies is right. Mom has been looking for him."

Jerry still wasn't happy about April being involved but trusted Max's intuition. He looked at Fred. "I think Max might have a lead on those guys we were talking about earlier. Unless there's been a major heist at the drawbridge, then she got a hit on a group of guys planning on pulling a smash and grab."

Max's eyes grew wide. "You mean you knew about them?"

Fred pulled out his notebook. "Do you know which drawbridge?"

Max shook her head.

"Did it lift or turn?" Fred asked.

"I think it turned. At least it did in my vision."

Fred smiled. "Centerville Turnpike."

Jerry relayed what Max had told him. "What do

you think? Could it be our guys?"

Fred looked over his notes. "Sure sounds like them. I'll get this to White."

"Wow, FBI. Cool."

Fred looked around the room and lowered his voice. "You know what's even cooler?"

Max leaned forward. "What?"

"You outrank him."

Max's eyes grew round. "Seriously?"

Fred nodded.

"What does it stand for?"

"What does what stand for?" Fred asked.

"NSA."

Jerry held up his hands when Fred looked at him. "This is the first I'm hearing of it."

Fred looked toward the stairs. "I think I'll go see what the rest of the household is up to. Join us when you can, okay?"

"We'll be right down," Jerry assured him.

"Did I make him mad?" Max asked once Fred was gone.

Jerry leaned forward and intertwined his hands. "You made him uncomfortable. People are used to their private thoughts staying private. Just because you can read a person doesn't mean you should. Nor should you tell them. It can lead to a lot of misunderstandings."

"You're not just talking about Fred, are you?"

"No, I'm not." Jerry sat back in his chair. "When

I was a young boy, I went snooping for the Christmas presents and found them hidden in a closet. I thought I was hot stuff because I already knew what I was getting. Only I wasn't, because Christmas morning, I knew everything under the tree, and there weren't any surprises."

"What about what Santa brought you?"

Jerry worked to keep his thoughts unreadable. "Yes, only what Santa brought. But in those days, Santa only brought one present. What I'm trying to say is you need some surprises in your life. Only pry if there is a reason, not just because you can."

Gunter raised his head and thumped the couch with his tail. Jerry looked to see April coming up the stairs. She smiled when she saw him and then turned her attention to Max. "Fred wants to see you downstairs."

"Am I in trouble?"

"No, why would you be in trouble? I think he just wants to see if you pick up on anything in the group posts."

Max pushed off the couch.

Gunter hesitated, then followed her down the stairs.

"Can we talk for a moment?" April asked as Jerry stood.

Jerry waved a hand toward the sitting area. "Sure, do you want to sit?"

"No, this won't take long. Besides, they want

you downstairs." She wrung her hands while she spoke. "Listen, Savannah told me she filled you in on what was said at the mall. I know you think a lot of Max, and you think she has everything all figured out. But she's still a kid – one with an extremely vivid imagination. I guess that's partially my fault because I force her to watch all those sappy movies with me. I can't tell you how many times we've watched *Mystic Pizza* together. Anyway, she's been without a dad for most of her life, and God knows Randy sure didn't show her any outpouring of fatherly love. Now you come along and are nice to her, and she sees what she wants to see. What I'm trying to tell you is that Max and I are fine, and we're going to continue to be fine. Especially now with the wonderful opportunity Max and I've been offered. It's a Godsend as we won't have time to be lonely. It's probably good that we don't have anyone to tie us down. I'm probably making a fool out of myself. I mean, it's not like there's any chemistry between us anyway, but if you were thinking there was, I just wanted to head you off. We are only here because Fred asked for us to come. We'll be going home soon, and Port Hope is a long way from..." April laughed. "Well, from everywhere."

Jerry felt her words in the pit of his stomach. *No chemistry? I could have sworn there was something there.* Jerry worked to hide his confusion. "It was quite the drive at that."

April turned toward the stairs. "I guess we'd better go see what the others are up to."

Jerry started to reach for her, but her words held him back. The last thing he wanted was to make a fool of himself. *It's not like there's any chemistry between us.* The phrase stuck in his heart like the blade of a knife and hurt even more than his cracked ribs. He slowed his pace to give her room and worked to regain his composure. The last thing he wanted was to force her to like him.

***

Jerry sat at the large dining room table, scrolling through the posts in the Facebook Strawberry Patch group. All eyes were on him as he read Susie's posts.

Hi, everyone,

Sorry I haven't posted for a while, but something happened a couple of months ago that really freaked me out. If you recall, my last post said I was working in Westerly, Rhode Island for the summer. Well, one night, I was walking home after a shift, and some bozo tried to kidnap me. I was able to get away, but it really freaked me out, so I took a break from social media for a while. I can still clearly see his face – mostly because I waited on the jerk at the pizza place where I worked before he tried to kidnap me. Seriously, what kind of loser shows his face before trying to nab someone? All I can say is if I ever see him again, I will know who he is. There's a jail cell with his name on it. I talk big, but I won't be going back to Westerly any time soon. Okay, so enough about my drama. I'm here in Virginia Beach, hanging out with my sister and some friends. So, come on, Reds, tell me, where are the best places for this redhead to visit?

A chill raced across the back of Jerry's neck. *She really antagonized the guy. No way was he not going to respond.* Jerry skimmed the comments, stopping on one with the username Star. *OMG, how scary. Glad you are alright. I hope they cut the guy's balls off. Anyhow, if you enjoy the beach, check out Ocean View Park. It's a lot less crowded since tourist season is over.* He looked up from the computer and focused on April. "Star?"

April frowned. "How'd you know?"

"It's my job to know." Jerry focused on the computer, reading the remaining comments. Most of them were similar to what April – Star – had posted. Jerry keyed on a woman named Ginger telling Susie she should check out First Landing State Park, saying if she was looking for privacy, it was far more secluded. Jerry turned the computer around and pointed to the comment. "This is him."

April beamed at her daughter. "That's the same one Max keyed on."

Susie pulled the computer closer and read aloud as she typed. "Cool! I hate crowds! It sounds like the perfect place. I have plans in the morning but will check it out after lunch. Hopefully, the water will still be warm enough to go in." She looked at Fred. "Should I post it?"

Jerry shook his head. "I don't like it."

Fred spoke up. "I know you have some misgivings, but the guy is more likely to show up if he thinks he has a chance at nabbing her without anyone seeing him."

Jerry stood his ground. "I've been to that park. It's too secluded."

"She won't be alone. She'll have us," April replied.

Jerry felt the hairs prickle on his neck. "You?"

"I'm going too," Max told him. "And Savannah too. We'll be able to feel if he's near."

Jerry glared at Fred. "What happened to keeping them out of it?"

"It was their plan. They had everything figured out when I got down here. It's a good plan. There are cabins on the beach, and my team can get there early and set up a command post."

Jerry pushed from his chair, and Gunter scrambled to his feet. "I don't like it. It's too dangerous."

Susie stood and looked him in the eye. "I'm not scared of him."

"You should be. You are exactly his type, plus you all but called him by name and told him you can identify him."

She had the audacity to laugh. "You do realize

the goal was to antagonize him, right? I fought him off once. I can do it again. I'm even better now, as I've been training."

"And this guy is pissed off. What if he changes his MO? What if he is so riled up, he doesn't care about being careful?"

"Are you trying to say this is a man's job? I hate to break it to you, Jerry, but you're not his type. You want this guy caught? I'm your gal, unless you don't think women are capable of protecting themselves?" There was a hardness about Susie that hadn't been there before. A wave of anger that radiated about her and dared anyone to get too close.

Jerry had no doubt she could protect herself under normal circumstances, but what if the guy decided not to play fair? He looked at April and then glanced at Max. What if he decided not to leave any witnesses? "I don't doubt you can take care of yourself as long as the guy sticks to his same routine. But what if he doesn't? What if this time he brings a gun? If you want to go through with this, I will back you up, but why have the others with you?"

Savannah, who'd been quiet until this point, cut in. "Oh no, you don't. You're not keeping me out of this. I didn't come to Virginia to sit on the sidelines."

"Me neither," April agreed. "Max can stay back, but I'm going."

Max jutted her chin. "I'm not staying home. I'll be able to feel him if he comes close. I'll know if he has a gun, and I can warn everyone."

Jerry slammed his fist on the table. Not understanding what all the yelling was about, Gunter entered the fray, barking and doing little hop-like steps.

Jerry ran his hand over his head and struggled to stay in control. "This is not a game."

Susie got in his face. "And we don't need your protection."

"Of course you do," Jerry told her.

"Because you're a chauvinist who doesn't think women can fight their own battles?"

"No, because I'm a Marine who made an oath to protect my country. I may not be a police officer anymore, but I made an oath to protect and serve. I'm a man who was raised by a mother and grandmother who taught me that women are to be cherished and protected. And above all that, I would do anything in my power to make sure that SOB never hurts another living soul. Do you have a problem with that, soldier?"

Susie stared at him for a moment and Jerry could feel some of her anger dissipating. "No, McNeal, I can't say that I do."

Chapter Eleven

Unable to sleep, Jerry was up and dressed by four a.m. He checked his pistol and shoved it in his waistband, then grabbed a pair of shorts and a shirt to change into later in the day. The aroma of coffee greeted him as he descended the stairs. He followed the smell, surprised to see the pot half empty. Fred was sitting in the breakfast room. Jerry smiled when he saw Gunter lying at the man's feet.

Jerry poured himself a cup and took the pot to the table. "Been up long?"

Fred leaned back in his chair, watching as Jerry refilled his cup. "For a while. Just sitting here alone in my thoughts."

"Not completely alone. Gunter is lying by your feet."

Fred looked at the floor. "What do you suppose that's about?"

Jerry walked the pot to the kitchen and placed it on the warmer. "Who knows? It could be that he likes you, or maybe he knew you were worried and came down here to send you calming vibes."

"He can do that?"

Jerry returned to the table and pulled out a chair. "He does it to me all the time. So, the big question is what's got you so worried, and don't say you're not."

"Our boy's a ghost." Fred sat his cup on the table. "Not in the literal sense, but a ghost all the same. We haven't been able to pinpoint a location where his posts are coming from. We can't find out where he lives or anything else about the guy. We've looked at hotel camera footage from everywhere we know he's been, and we have nothing. If you still have misgivings about sending them out there today, we can scratch the plan."

That Fred was nervous made Jerry feel better. It meant he didn't think this was a slam-dunk case and, therefore, would take every precaution to ensure nothing was left to chance. "It's a good plan. We'll run with it. I'll be there, and so will Max and Savannah. Between us using our intuition and your guys hiding in the wings, we'll get him."

"Why the turnaround? Last night, you were adamant it was a bad idea."

Last night, I'd just been stabbed in the gut and was not thinking clearly. Jerry let that piece of the puzzle remain hidden. He took a sip of his coffee. "Last night, I let Susie's energy get the better of me. What I saw was a woman pig-headed enough to think she could fight off a killer with her own bare hands."

Fred raised an eyebrow. "Have you seen her arms? She might just be able to do it."

Jerry smiled his agreement but shook his head to the contrary. "Could she do it? Probably. But her energy was all wrong. She's scared."

"Being scared is a good thing?" Fred questioned.

"A very good thing. It will keep her on her toes. When people think they have all the answers, they get sloppy. When they are scared, all of their senses are on high alert and could just mean the difference between someone living and dying." Jerry thought of Manning and the chances he used to take. The man was cocky and almost got himself killed.

Gunter yawned a squeaky yawn.

Jerry decided to change the subject. "What time are we setting up?"

"Barney has had a team in the park since midnight. We've got three cabins and placed some cameras in the trees. We'll have others throughout the park and a helicopter on standby in case of an emergency. If our guy shows, he won't get away. I'll be in one of the cabins with a team monitoring the cameras. You know what works for you, so we'll leave you to it." Fred flicked a finger toward the kitchen.

Jerry looked to see Susie standing at the coffee pot.

She poured herself a cup and held up the pot. "Anyone need a refill?"

Jerry lifted his cup.

Susie walked to the table, filled Jerry's cup, then topped off Fred. "Is this a private party, or can anyone join?"

Fred waved a hand to the empty chairs. "Be our guest."

"Let me put on a fresh pot first. This one's had it." She walked to the sink, filled the pot with water, and started another pot before making her way back to the table. She looked at Jerry. "Sorry for last night. I didn't mean to come off acting like …"

"Like someone who's had their whole life turned upside down?" Jerry finished for her.

She smiled and took a drink. "I need to get this guy. I haven't slept worth a wink since all this started."

"We'll get him," Jerry promised.

"Today?"

Jerry nodded. "Feels that way."

"The weather's agreeable today. It's supposed to hit 83."

"Good thing I remembered to bring my bikini."

Fred grinned, and Jerry laughed. "Take it easy, soldier. You're going to give the old man heart palpitations."

Fred drained his cup. "Speak for yourself. I have the heart of a young man."

"That he keeps in a jar on his desk," Jerry added.

Fred smiled a sly smile. "Yes, it belongs to the

last wiseacre that insulted me. I've always thought about getting a brain to keep it company."

From his place on the floor, Gunter growled a soft growl.

Jerry stood and leaned in close to whisper in Fred's ear. "You'll have to get past the dog first."

Gunter stood and leaned against Fred's leg. Fred's eyes grew wide, and his words came out in an excited whisper. "I felt him!" His face paled. "He's not going to bite me, is he? Tell him I was just kidding about cutting out your brain."

"Not unless you give him a reason." Jerry looked at Susie, and his voice turned serious. "I'm going to head out for a bit. If I'm not back before you leave, be safe out there. You may or may not see me, but I'll be there."

Susie stood and kissed him on the cheek. "Thanks, Jerry."

"No need to thank me. We will get this guy. Just make sure you don't take any unnecessary chances." Jerry looked at Fred. "I'm feeling a bit stir-crazy. I'm going to take a drive and see what comes through. I'll be in contact."

Jerry was almost to the front door when Gunter gave a yip. He turned to see Max hurrying down the stairs.

"Where are you going, Jerry?"

"Out for a bit. I want to see if I can get a feel for things."

"Can I go with you?"

"No." He smiled. "I'd rather you stay close to your mom today. She really wants to help find this guy, and I want to make sure she doesn't get overlooked."

Max scrunched up her nose. "What do you mean?"

"I mean, everyone is going to be concentrating on Susie. I need to know someone is watching over your mom too. I think you are perfectly capable of keeping your senses focused on both."

"But you'll be there too, won't you, Jerry?"

"You know it, kiddo," Jerry promised. "And, Max?"

"Yes?"

"If you need anything or feel unsafe at any point, just think of Gunter, and he will be there. Isn't that right, boy?"

Gunter jumped up, placed his paws on Max's shoulders, and slathered her with K-9 kisses.

Max giggled with delight before finally motioning him down.

Jerry lifted her chin with his finger. "Promise me you'll watch yourself out there."

Max nodded. "I promise."

Jerry released her chin and placed his hand alongside her cheek. "Good. I'll see you and your mom later." He turned and left without another word.

Gunter was waiting in the passenger seat when he opened the door. While a part of him wished the dog was staying with Max, a larger part was pleased the dog had chosen to ride along. Jerry didn't have a destination in mind but was surprised when the pull had him going south on 168 instead of north. As he drove, the pull intensified. "No, it can't be today. I don't have time for this."

Gunter's ear twitched as if he, too, felt the energy in the air.

Jerry had nearly reached the Edinburgh exit when he saw a large black SUV idling in the emergency lane just before a sign that read "Coming Soon: Custom Homes." Across the field, Jerry could see the subdivision he and Fred had toured. He tried to get a look at the driver, but the guy had his head turned away from the road. As soon as Jerry passed the SUV, the tingling eased. Jerry chided himself for not getting a better look at the driver. He took the exit, doubled back around and saw that the SUV was still there. He'd hoped to go up a mile or so and cross over the center median, something he was unable to do as there was a fence preventing such maneuvers. He pressed on the gas, racing to the next exit, then retraced his route, only to find the SUV no longer sitting beside the road.

Jerry hit his hand on the wheel. "Good one, McNeal. Not even so much as a license plate." He took the exit and drove back to the subdivision, going through once in search of the SUV. Not finding it, he took another lap much slower as he mentally documented what he saw – all of the homes were brick, with the vast majority having three to five garage doors. The entrances were grand, most having double entrance doors – something he particularly disliked as he didn't feel they were safe, as most gave way to open entryways and had no way of preventing the door from being kicked in. The neighborhood felt welcoming. Then again, that could just be due to the oversized stamped sidewalks that led the way to the front entrances – most of which had festive fall mums and pumpkins, making the stately homes fit for the cover of a magazine. Each lawn was perfectly manicured with not so much as a newspaper on the driveway. No, this neighborhood had boxes for that purpose. Struthers had said the gang preferred to smash and grab. Jerry had no doubt this neighborhood was on their list, but he'd yet to figure out how they would manage to rob more than one house without neighbors calling to alert their friends.

Unless they had a specific target in mind, they would need to hit as many houses as they could in as short a time as possible. Since there was only one way in and out of the subdivision, their attack would have to be quick and well-orchestrated.

Jerry drummed his fingers on the steering wheel. "Talk to me, boys. What's your plan?" He'd no sooner asked the question when he saw a black SUV coming up behind him. Jerry pulled to the curb and craned his neck to see the driver when the SUV drove around. *No joy.*

The SUV pulled into a driveway, and a woman got out, taking with her what looked to be a witch costume. *You blew this one, McNeal. You'd better not let that be the theme of the day. There are a lot of people counting on you.* Jerry looked at the time as he let his foot off the brake and headed out of the subdivision. He stopped at the stop sign at the corner of Edinburgh Parkway and Scone Castle Loop. Jerry took out his phone and pulled up the photo Max had drawn of the killer. He used his fingers to zoom in on the man's face and willed his gift to take over. *I know you're out here. Where are you hiding?* As Jerry looked up, he saw a black skeleton running across the field. He blinked, and the skeleton was gone. He snuck a glance at Gunter, who didn't appear to see anything that concerned him. Jerry skimmed the field that bordered a small pond once more before making his turn.

***

The pull took him to Virginia Beach to the Hollydaze Inn parking lot. There'd been a time when the name of the inn would have provoked a smile, but now it only managed to remind him of the inner turmoil that was a constant way of life of late. Jerry had yet to open the email Holly had sent him and wasn't sure if he ever would. He pushed thoughts of Holly from his mind and went inside the hotel. While the pull was there, it wasn't as strong as he thought it would be. *He's not here.* No, but he had been recently; of that, Jerry was sure. He stood in the lobby, feeling the energy. The elevator doors chimed, and Jerry hurried to catch it. He waited for the door to close and pushed every button.

Gunter tilted his head and yawned a grumbling yawn.

"What? How else am I going to figure out what floor he used?"

Gunter jumped up and pawed at the fifth-floor button.

"Show off."

Gunter lifted his lip.

The elevator stopped on the second floor. The door opened, and Jerry stepped into the hall. Not feeling anything, he ducked back inside the box just as the door began to close. He did the same on the third floor and was getting ready to repeat the process when the elevator settled on the fourth floor.

The door opened, and a man wearing a gray suit stepped inside carrying a briefcase. He smiled a greeting. "I figure I can either stand in the hall or go for a ride. What goes up must come down, right?" The man glanced at the control panel and frowned when he saw that all the upper-floor buttons were lit up. He looked at Jerry.

Jerry shrugged. "I was bored."

"Next time, take the stairs," the man grumbled and moved to the opposite side.

Jerry decided to take the man's advice and stepped out of the elevator when the door opened to the fifth floor.

Gunter followed him into the hall.

Instantly, Jerry's senses were on high alert. He took a right and hurried down the hall. The floor was quiet, the only noise coming from a vacuum cleaner in one of the nearby rooms. Jerry stopped short of the cleaning cart and placed his hand on the door to room 514.

"It works better with a key."

Jerry swiveled to see a hotel cleaning lady pulling linens from the cart.

Jerry took a chance. "The thing of it is, I kind of already checked out. But I forgot to get my razor out of the shower."

She reached into the cart and pulled out a plastic razor. "I've got extras."

"No, this one was electric. Cordless," Jerry added when she frowned. "It was a gift from my grandmother. I'd really hate to lose it."

"I'm not really supposed to do this." She checked to make sure no one was looking before opening the door and going into the bathroom.

Jerry followed. *So trusting, and the killer was here not too long ago. I'm glad she isn't a redhead.*

He scanned the room, moving out of the way just before she turned.

"Are you sure this is the right room?" she asked.

"I'm sure of it. Maybe I left it in one of the drawers." He hurried across the room and pulled open each drawer in turn. *Something's not right. This is the room, I'm sure of it, and yet I don't feel him anywhere but the bathroom.*

Even Gunter contained his sniffing to the section of the room closest to the door.

Jerry ran a hand over his head.

"Maybe you should check your suitcase again," the woman suggested.

Jerry smiled. "You're probably right. I'm sure I packed it and just don't remember."

Jerry hurried to the elevator and pushed the button.

Gunter barked and looked to the stairs. Jerry shook his head. "You can take them if you want, but the guy with the cracked ribs prefers to ride."

The elevator dinged. The door slid open, and Jerry found himself face to face with the man who'd joined him when the elevator stopped on the fourth floor.

Jerry stepped inside, breathing a sigh of relief when Gunter followed.

The man scowled at him. "Touch any of those buttons, and I'll break your finger."

Chapter Twelve

Jerry slipped into the bathroom at the hotel and changed into his shorts and t-shirt. He debated taking off his rib brace but knew he could move with less pain while wearing the brace. He stopped and picked up a cheap beach umbrella, a beach chair, and a printed towel that clearly shouted tourist. At the last moment, he added a ball cap and sunblock and picked up a sailing magazine. Next, he stopped at 7-Eleven and purchased a small bag of ice and a six-pack of beer. He drove to a vacant lot, poured out half, then placed the empty cans and the remaining beers into the small cooler he always carried with him before covering everything with ice.

Fred called just as he was getting back in the truck. Jerry answered the call. "Yep."

"We're all set up. The ladies will be pulling into the parking lot in fifteen minutes. We have a tail on them that will break off the moment they pull in. The gate guard is one of ours, and we'll have eyes on them from the moment they enter the park. I told them they should go to the beach and stay there, so they are out in the open. If the guy shows up, we've got him."

"He'll show. My senses have been on full alert all morning. Speaking of which, we need to set up a meeting with White and his guys. I've got something for them."

"Care to share?"

"No, I haven't fit all the pieces into the puzzle just yet."

"But you will by tomorrow."

"Things are taking shape, so it shouldn't be much longer."

"That is one heck of a brain you have there, McNeal."

"You can't have my brain, Fred." Jerry laughed when Gunter emitted a growl. "Gunter wants me to tell you he has an eye on you."

"Tell the dog we have eyes on you both. That is you that just pulled in, isn't it?"

"Yep."

"Good, don't forget to pay the man at the gate."

"Not one of the fringe benefits of the job?"

"On any other day, yes. But since we don't know where this guy is, you are just an ordinary guy heading to the beach. Hey. You don't suppose you can get the dog to show himself for today, do you?"

"Why's that?"

"It would look more natural if you had a dog."

Jerry glanced at Gunter, knowing this was just Fred's way of finally seeing the dog. "Nice try."

"I don't know what you're talking about."

Jerry stopped at the guard booth, handed the man a ten, and waited for his change.

"Fred said I'm supposed to charge extra for the dog."

Jerry lowered his back window. "I don't see a dog, do you?"

The guy ducked his head through the window and shook his head. "I guess Fred was trying to pull one over on me."

Jerry smiled. "I reckon so."

The guy handed him his change. "Have a nice day."

"You too." Jerry parked and walked to the visitor center to have a look around. Not seeing or feeling anything out of the ordinary, he returned to the Durango, grabbed his cooler and supplies, then picked his way to the beach. He chose a spot just to the left of the main path back to the parking lot, knowing the ladies would see him when they made their way to the beach. He stabbed the umbrella into the sand, then unfolded his chair, turning it so he could see both the beach and catch new arrivals out of his peripheral vision. He spread out the towel and placed the cooler beside the chair. He sat, rooted around in the cooler, and pulled out one of the empty cans, sticking his finger into the tab and making a show of opening it before tilting it back. After a moment, he tossed the can onto the towel and reached for another one.

His cell rang. Jerry looked at Gunter. "I'll bet you an ice cream cone that's Uncle Fred."

Gunter licked his lips as Jerry pulled his phone from his pocket. "Hello?"

"Better take it easy on the brewskies there, McNeal. What were you saying about everyone keeping their wits about them?"

"Relax, boss, I'm just putting on a show. The cans are already empty."

"Yeah, I knew that."

"Sure you did."

"Speaking of playing the part. You definitely look like a tourist. Those just might be the whitest legs I've ever had the displeasure of seeing."

"Yeah, I'm not much of a short-pants guy."

"No, I'm saying it's a good thing. No way will the killer think you're a local."

Before Jerry could answer, a message popped up from Barney. *> Don't let him fool you, his legs are just as white.*

Gunter stood and stared toward the parking lot, wagging his tail.

"Max is here."

"Those are some good powers you've got there."

"Nah, the dog gets all the credit for this one. Time to go to work. Let's nail this dirtbag." Jerry ended the call but kept the phone to his ear as he turned to Gunter. "Keep your eyes open, boy. It's time to put a bad guy away for a very long time."

Jerry felt their presence even before hearing their excited chatter. It occurred to him this was Max and April's first trip to the ocean. The thought both excited and saddened him as the experience would always be marred by the memory of why they were here. They weren't here to enjoy a holiday; they were here to help catch a killer. Jerry sighed.

His sadness was short-lived.

"A dolphin! Do you see it, Mom?"

Come on, Max, remember your part. You're supposed to live in the area, remember.

"I know I've seen them before, but I never get tired of seeing them."

Jerry smiled. He wasn't sure if she'd picked up on his thought or if her mother had reminded her of her part. It didn't matter. *That a girl, Max.*

Jerry sat leafing through his magazine.

Susie and the others started to his left, and Jerry gave the slightest of nods. *Go the other way. I won't be able to see you in that direction.*

Gunter raced to Max and tugged her in the opposite direction. Max took the hint, walking through the sand with her head down. She stopped about five hundred feet from where he sat and waved her arm. "Over here, Mom. There's less seaweed on this side."

Jerry wasn't sure if there was seaweed on the other side, but it worked, as April, Susie and

Savannah swerved and walked to where Max was standing. Though their voices were light and calm, the energy that surrounded them swirled about them like a dark cloud.

Jerry drew in a breath when Susie pulled her sundress over her head, revealing an impressively toned body beneath the tiniest of lime-green bikinis. *She looks like Christmas. And oh, what a package.* Jerry saw April looking in his direction and lowered his head, pretending to be engrossed in his magazine while covertly watching the show. Susie kicked off her flip-flops, ran to the water's edge, and picked up a shell. When she did, most of the back of her swimsuit disappeared.

Jerry reached for the cooler. This time, he pulled out a full can, pulled the tab, and drank as the movie *Cool Hand Luke* came to mind. The men in the scene were working on a chain gang as a voluptuous woman proceeded to wash her vehicle in a highly seductive way. One of the men commented about how she didn't know what she was doing, to which another assured him she knew full well what it was she was doing. It was the same with Susie. She knew she was there to tease and torment her attacker into action, and she was doing a fine job of it. He could only imagine the comments of those looking on.

Jerry rolled his neck and casually checked his surroundings. When he looked again, Savannah and April had removed their coverups. While Savannah wore a bikini, hers covered most of what it was supposed to cover. Jerry was pleased to see that while April could have easily carried off wearing a bikini, she had opted to cover herself in a one-piece that looked both sexy and helped leave something to the imagination. She saw him looking and smiled.

Jerry's phone chimed. He clicked on a message from Fred. > *Put your tongue back in your mouth. You're practically drooling.*

Jerry typed his reply. > *Last I checked, I'm not married.* He looked at April and sighed. *Nor am I in a commitment.*

Fred> *No, but you are working. Just making sure you're not getting sidetracked.*

Jerry took off his hat and ran his hand over his head, lifting his middle finger in the process. He heard Max giggle and replaced his cap. Though Max hadn't seen the gesture, it reminded him of his promise to curtail his language. Jerry picked up the magazine. This time, he actually read what was on the pages.

***

Though Jerry was used to being alone, sitting here on the beach for the last few hours had him feeling like a voyeur. Though he knew the time was near, he also knew there was no immediate danger. He tilted his hat over his eyes, knowing his senses would tell him when trouble was close by. Max and the others seemed to share his assessment as they swam and played in the water.

Jerry's phone chimed. Fred> *We have a guy heading up from your left. Not sure where he came from, but it wasn't through the front gate.*

Jerry> *I'm on it.* Jerry set the magazine under the leg of his chair and started walking toward the guy. Gunter ran ahead of him, sniffed the man in question, then returned to Jerry. Though the guy's build seemed to be right, nothing alerted his senses. Nor did he match the man in Max's drawing. The further he got from his chair, the less his neck tingled. Jerry reached into the sand as if picking up a shell, then circled back to his chair. He pulled out his phone. *>Not our guy.*

Fred> *I figured that when you didn't take him down.*

Jerry resisted the urge to remove his hat once more.

Five minutes later, Jerry's phone rang, showing a call from Fred. Jerry answered it. "Yes?"

"We may have trouble. There are four women heading toward the beach."

Jerry kept his voice low. "Any of them driving a white van?"

"Nope."

"Then what's the problem?"

"They're all redheads."

As soon as the words came out of Fred's mouth, Jerry's radar was on full alert. "Crap."

"That's precisely what I was thinking. Barney suggested that some of the girls from the group got together and decided to come and surprise Susie."

Jerry sighed. "Sounds plausible."

It didn't take long for the small group of bathing beauties to make it to the beach and make a beeline for Susie and the others. Susie emerged from the water and hugged them each in turn as if greeting long-lost friends.

Jerry watched Max's body language to see if she picked up on anything. If she did, it didn't show. The girls kicked off their shoes and joined Susie and the others in the water. Even Gunter joined the fun, running amongst the women before finally giving in to his love of the water and going for a swim.

It was well after four when Jerry's cell chimed with another message from Fred. >*Looks like we have a couple of stragglers.*

Jerry blew out a sigh and typed in his reply. > *Unless they're driving a white van, I don't care.*

Only he did care, as he thought the killer would have shown himself by now. And if no one had eyes on the man, why was his radar now pinging as if the guy was right on top of him? He heard voices and turned to see two women with red hair walking toward the beach. The shorter of the two wore a one-piece bathing suit, while the other, taller woman wore a flowing skirt and loose-fitting blouse. The woman's eyes were heavily made up, and she wore brilliant red lipstick that nearly matched her hair. She carried a caddy with two bottles of wine in one hand and her sandals in the other. *A bit overdressed, aren't we?*

As if hearing him, the woman looked in his direction and smiled a flirty smile. Her gaze dropped to the empty beer cans, and she turned away.

There was something about her that had his radar pinging. Maybe it was the way she looked at him as if drinking beer out of a can classified him as a neanderthal or that she was dressed way too classy for a day at the beach.

Don't go reading too much into it, McNeal. If she wants to look pretty on the beach, what's the big deal? You've met plenty of women who wouldn't step outside the house without putting on makeup. Jerry drummed his fingers on the chair. *Maybe that's it. Or, maybe I'm pinging on her because she caught the eye of the Hash Mark Killer.* Jerry felt the skin on the back of his neck crawl – if he were hooked to a siren, it would be blaring. *He's here.*

Jerry stood and scanned the beach, looking for any sign of the man. *Nothing. Don't blow it, Jerry.* He sat back down, trying his best to act casual.

The woman with the wine started in his direction. Halfway to him, April joined her. Max ran out of the water and called to April.

Something's wrong. Max feels it too. Jerry strained to hear what they were saying. Whatever it was, Max didn't like it. He could tell by the way she crossed her arms and stomped her foot. April pointed toward the blanket. Max stayed rooted in place. The woman in the dress said something, and April laughed as they started walking again. Max followed at a distance.

April slid a glance toward him and shrugged. "Kids. They think they need to follow you everywhere. We are just going to Trudy's car to get the wine glasses she forgot."

Jerry was grateful to April for telling him where she was going, but he wasn't happy she wasn't listening to Max. Especially since Jerry now felt trouble all around them. While his heart told him to follow April, he wasn't sure if it was instinct or his need to protect the woman. Fred and his team would be close to April and the woman once they reached the parking lot, but if Jerry left, he would be leaving the rest of the women vulnerable. He was still watching after April when Max ran up.

Tears in her eyes, she grabbed hold of his arm. "Where's your phone?"

Jerry frowned. "In my pocket. Why?"

Max's eyes were darting back and forth, and Jerry could feel her trembling. "Call her."

"What do you mean call her? She's right there. I can just go to her."

Max clawed into his arm. "NO! Call her. Do it now!"

"Okay. Max, calm down. I'll call her." Jerry reached for his phone, found April's number, and pressed dial. "There, see, I'm calling her."

The sound of bells drifted through the air and then grew louder. Jerry recognized the tune as ACDC's "Hell's Bells." *Bells.* Jerry looked at Max. She nodded. Jerry ran, his bare feet sinking into the sand and his ribs aching with every step. He struggled to increase his speed as the woman in the dress grabbed hold of April's arm and began dragging her up the path.

Suddenly, Gunter appeared in front of them. Wearing his police vest, the K-9 bared his teeth as he stood blocking their way.

The woman tried to use April as a shield to get past Gunter. The dog lunged, grabbing hold of her arm. She tried to get away, and April snatched a handful of hair.

Jerry was just getting to the wooden pathway when the hair let go from the woman's scalp.

A wig! *It's him.* The killer pushed April toward Gunter and turned, running straight toward Jerry.

He saw Jerry, and a look of relief washed over his face. "Help, there's a rabid dog after me!"

Jerry caught his breath, doubled up his fist, and rammed it straight into the man's ruby-red lips. The guy's forehead creased, and he fell backward without a sound.

Gunter hovered over him, daring him to move. Not likely, as the man was out cold.

Chapter Thirteen

Fred's team swarmed the path like locusts. Jerry stepped back to give them room as Susie, Savannah, and the others ran up from the beach.

Susie pushed through the crowd. She glared at the man, who was now sitting in the back of an unmarked car. "It's him. Even with the makeup, I'm certain."

Fred nodded to Barney. "By the book, and make sure to read him his rights."

Susie walked to the edge of the parking lot, where she was embraced by several of her fellow redheads. Not having any words of wisdom to offer, Jerry left them alone.

Savannah stood off to the side with her arms crossed around her. Jerry walked over to her. She gave him a weak smile. "I guess you didn't need me here after all."

Jerry tilted his head. "Why, because you didn't nab the guy?"

Savannah nodded. "I didn't even help."

Jerry chuckled. "Don't beat yourself up about it. I was within feet of the guy and had no clue he wasn't a woman."

"Yes, but I'll bet you knew something was up."

"I did. But honestly, I probably would have blown it if I'd acted alone."

Savannah brushed a strand of hair from her mouth. "How's that?"

"I knew something was up, but I thought I was pinging on the next victim. If not for Max, I'm certain I would have approached him and warned him about the killer. The guy would have known we were onto him and probably disappeared for good." Jerry nodded toward Max, standing by her mom as she gave her statement. "She's the real hero. Maybe you should give yourself a pat on the back instead of beating yourself up."

"Why's that?"

"Because you're the one that's been working with her. We all have our own gifts, Savannah. Maybe yours is making sure everyone else can fully understand theirs. You remind me of Granny in some ways."

Savannah's face brightened. "I do? How?"

"She could read cards and tea leaves and see spirits after they crossed. We could communicate without talking, but she didn't get the feeling, not the way I do. She always said it was her calling to help me with my gifts. And she did, the best she could anyway."

Savannah smiled a forgiving smile. "Thanks,

Jerry. You always know the right thing to say. I'm going to go check on Susie."

"Okay, if I don't talk to you again, I'll see you back at the house." Jerry looked for April and saw she was still talking to the detectives – just as well, as he wasn't ready to speak to her, since he was still angry at her for diverting from the plan.

Max saw him standing alone and ran over to him. "We got him, Jerry! We really did it."

Jerry smiled. "I think it's fair to say you did it. How did you know to put the ringtone in your mom's phone?"

"Granny told me."

"Granny?" Jerry blinked his surprise. "My Granny?"

Max nodded. "She came into my room after you left and told me I had to put the bells in Mom's phone. I didn't know what she meant, so she showed me the song. Granny told me you had to be the one to call her and that it would keep her safe. She was right."

"She usually is." Jerry looked to the sky. *Thank you, Granny.* "Hey, it looks like your mom's done. I'm sure she'll want to go home. Do you want to go with her?"

Max shook her head. "No, she's pretty upset and will probably just want to take a nap. Savannah and Susie will be with her. Can I stay with you?"

"Sure you can, kiddo. As long as your mom says

it's alright."

"Okay, I'll go ask."

Jerry watched Max run off, then waved a hand to get Fred's attention. "Make sure someone follows April and the others to see they get home safe. I'm taking Max with me. I want to drive by the drawbridge and see what kind of feeling we get."

Fred frowned. "Don't you think you should rest up a bit?"

Jerry laughed. "I said I was driving by it, not diving off of it. Tell April I'll see her when I get back to the house."

Fred looked over his shoulder. "She's right over there. Why don't you tell her?"

Jerry shook his head. "I'm not ready to talk to her just yet."

Fred lifted an eyebrow. "Is this one of those lovers' quarrels?"

"This is one of those 'I'm afraid I'll say something I may live to regret' things." Jerry sighed. "Dang it, Fred, the woman knew how dangerous it was. What was she thinking?"

Fred shrugged. "According to her, she was trying to protect Max. She couldn't tell the woman was a guy. Heck, me and the boys are ready to gouge our eyes out for the thoughts we had when we saw her walking down to the beach. A few even remarked as to wanting to see what she was hiding under that skirt. I assure you, no one guessed that right. You were within feet of her and couldn't tell. She – he made up some excuse about forgetting the wine glasses, and April was worried about her walking alone. When you do talk to her, cut her a little slack. She wasn't trying to be a hero. She was just being nice."

"Why April?" Jerry asked. "She doesn't fit the profile. The killer – do we have a name?"

"Rudy Foster, if what he's telling us is true."

"Susie was right there. Why take April?"

Fred eyed Max. "My guess, and this is only a guess, Rudy was hoping to make a trade. Maybe he got there and saw he wouldn't be able to get close to Susie, so he took April instead. Probably thought he could take April somewhere and have her call Susie with some excuse as to why they left and have her meet them, and then take both out, so there were no witnesses."

"That'd probably be my guess as well," Jerry agreed, knowing how close he'd come to losing her.

Fred scratched at his head. "My question is, why did he let her go?"

"What do you mean?"

"We knew something was up by the way you were acting. Then when you started running, I gave the go. He had April and could have used her as a hostage, but instead, he started running the other way and right into your fist. Good takedown, by the way. But it just doesn't make sense as to why he started running in the first place."

Jerry looked at Fred and grinned. "You'd run too if you were being threatened by the ghost of a ninety-pound police dog."

Fred's jaw dropped. "Rudy can see him? You're telling me that SOB has the gift?"

Jerry shook his head. "He doesn't have the gift. Gunter was all over the guy when they were loading him into the car, and he never reacted."

"Then how could he see him at the time?"

"Because Gunter wanted to be seen." Jerry held up a hand when Fred started to speak. "Don't ask me how, because I don't know. He just does it. When he needs or wants to be seen, he can."

Fred looked around. "Is he here now?"

Jerry pointed a finger to where Gunter was sitting, staring up at Fred. "He's sitting right there."

"Tell him I need to see him."

"You just did."

"What did he say?"

Jerry smiled. "He's a dog, Fred. Dogs don't talk."

Fred heaved a sigh. "He's not going to show himself to me, is he?"

Gunter lifted his lip, showing a K-9 grin. Jerry knew the dog was enjoying this game with his newfound friend. "Probably not."

Fred looked at his phone when it buzzed. "Got to go. I want to be there when they question this guy.

You sure you don't want to come along?"

Absolutely not. Jerry shook his head. "I haven't lost anything in that interrogation room."

"Aren't you even the slightest bit curious as to his motive?" Fred asked, rocking back on his heels.

Jerry felt his jaw twitch. "I couldn't give a crap about his motive. Why should it matter if he has mommy issues or daddy issues? Or if he thinks he was doing them a favor because he thinks redheads have no souls. What he did was atrocious. The man needs to be sent away for life."

Fred clamped Jerry on his shoulder. "We'll do our part, McNeal. That I can promise you."

***

Jerry stood at the side of the road waiting for traffic to pass. Once the road was clear, he, Max, and Gunter walked to the center of the road. Jerry turned to Max. "Take me through it again."

She nodded. "The gates are down, and there are cars here waiting."

"How many cars?"

"Six."

"What kind?"

She shrugged.

Think, Jerry. "Okay, are they SUVs, vans, or trucks? Do you see the color?"

"White SUV, like yours, only not as loud. Minivan – silver. Another minivan – red. A small black car. Another SUV – black. And a green

Volkswagen." She smiled. "I know what those look like."

Jerry keyed on the VW. "The Volkswagen, is it old or new?"

"Old, like in the *Lovebug* movie." She shrugged. "Mom likes the classics."

Gunter barked.

Jerry looked to see a line of cars coming and motioned them to the side of the road. "That's good, Max. Very good. You said they came from the ditch. What side?"

"Both."

Jerry looked at the water that filled the ditch behind them. "How did they do it without getting wet?"

Max concentrated on his question. "They're wearing some kind of suits."

"Like wet suits?"

"No. More like green camo that the hunters use."

"How many guys?"

"Twelve. One for each side of the car. And the bad guy."

"So thirteen. They're all doing bad things. Why do you call him the bad guy?"

"Because he's there to shoot anyone who doesn't listen."

"What do you mean who doesn't listen?"

"If they don't give money or do what they are supposed to do." She shrugged. "I don't know. I just know he's the bad guy. He shoots people."

"I need to know when this is going to happen. Can you tell me that?"

She closed her eyes for a moment. "Halloween."

"Halloween. Are you sure?"

Max nodded. "Yep."

"How can you tell?"

"Because they are wearing masks."

"You mean the bad guys are wearing masks," Jerry corrected.

"No, the kids in the back of the van. They're wearing costumes and masks and have bags of candy."

As soon as she said it, everything made sense. Struthers had told them they came in like a wrecking ball and did their smash and grabs on the same day. "Of course. Hitting the bridge on Halloween makes sense. They will hit the houses on the same day!"

"What houses?"

"The ones I keyed on the other day. I was trying to figure out how they would do it, but your vision gave me my answer. Halloween. It is the one day everyone turns into the most trusting individuals on the planet. And the one day people readily open their doors to complete strangers. The robbers wouldn't have to break the doors in. They would just need to make sure they couldn't be shut in their face when the homeowner realizes what is going on. What better way than to choose homes with double entry doors?"

"Why double doors?"

Jerry realized he'd been thinking out loud. "A house with double doors is more likely to have an open entryway."

"And that's a good thing, right?"

"It is if you want to have a grand entrance. But not if you want to keep safe."

"Because there are two doors?"

"No, because there's nothing to brace the doors. If someone wants to come in, they just have to put their shoulder into it and push. You can do that with single doors too. But sometimes, those homes have a way to brace the door. Okay, we know the where and the why. Now we need to know how they get away without being caught. For instance, the guys get into the black SUV, which would have to be pretty big to fit twelve guys. Do they speed through the opening the moment the gates go up?"

"No, they back up."

"All the way down the road?"

"No, just to that sign."

Gunter looked in the direction she was pointing and barked his agreement.

Jerry peered at the yellow sign. It wouldn't be hard to do, as there wouldn't be any vehicles in the other lane. Someone who knew how to back up a vehicle could do so without interference, turn when they got the chance, and speed off into the sunset.

"Maxine Buchanan. You sure are some kid."

"You know, Jerry. My name doesn't sound so bad when you say it."

Jerry sighed. "What say we go check on your mom and see how she's doing?"

***

April was sitting alone in the upper lounge when they returned. Max hugged her, made sure she was okay and headed to the pool.

Jerry watched Gunter follow her down the stairs, then turned to April. "Why aren't you in the pool?"

"I think I've had enough water for today."

Jerry gave a nod to the couch. "Mind if I join you?"

April tucked her feet further under her bottom. "Please do."

Jerry could tell by her red-rimmed eyes that she'd been crying. "Are you okay?"

Fresh tears sprang to her eyes, and she pulled a tissue from the box on the table beside her. "I was until you asked."

"It's okay to cry. It's when you keep things inside that you have a problem."

"You sound like a shrink."

He chuckled. "I should. I've seen enough of them."

She sniffed. "You have?"

Another chuckle. "I was pretty messed up for a while."

"Must not have been too bad if they let you be a cop."

"I wasn't suicidal or homicidal, so I guess they felt I was fit for the job."

"You looked pretty upset at the park."

No use hiding it, McNeal. "I was."

"I thought…"

Jerry cut her off. "Fred told me."

"Trudy said she forgot the wine glasses and that we should toast Susie's newfound confidence. She seemed so genuine."

"Which is probably how he managed to get away with killing all those women. Several of the victims said the same thing."

April shivered.

"Are you cold?"

"No, I was just thinking that you could be sitting here talking to my ghost."

A chill raced up his spine. "I'm glad I'm not."

"Me too. Jerry, would you mind holding me? Nothing else. Just hold me in your arms so I can feel safe?" Without waiting for him to answer, she turned and pressed into his side.

Jerry wrapped his arms around her. As he sat there holding her, he couldn't help thinking, for two people who didn't have any chemistry, they sure fit together rather well.

Chapter Fourteen

Jerry pulled into the Target parking lot, headed to the back of the lot, backed into the space next to White's SUV, and rolled down the window. White got out and handed Jerry a large cup of coffee.

"Fred's been detained." Jerry removed the lid, sniffed the contents then returned the cap before taking a sip.

"Fine, I'll drink his. I heard you caught the man. Got enough to hold him?"

"Yep."

"I sure hope you're right."

If not, there are other options. Jerry motioned Gunter to the back and looked at White. "Hop in. I want to show you something."

White hesitated. "That dog in there?"

Jerry sighed. "Fred's got a big mouth."

"Your secret's safe with me. I'll tell you, though, it was hard keeping a straight face when Struthers told me about the meeting with you two."

Jerry smiled. "Is that why he didn't come?"

White climbed inside the passenger seat. "You wouldn't get him in the same car with either of you at gunpoint. The man thinks you two have cooties or something. He probably took multiple showers when he got home. What'd you do to him anyway?"

"Say hello to Mr. White, boy." Jerry watched as Gunter leaned forward and licked the man's ear.

White's hand flew to his ear. "What was that?"

Jerry chuckled. "Struthers' so-called cooties. The dog licked your ear."

"Hmm, it felt like something was crawling on my ear. I can't tell you how many times I've felt that. Does that mean I've encountered spirits before?"

"Most people have and don't have a clue."

"Interesting. Where are we going?" White asked.

"I'm going to show you the first target."

White raised an eyebrow. "The first?"

"We know of two. I don't know if it will be the same crew or if they have more than one team. That will be for you to find out." Jerry drove to Edinburgh Meadows subdivision and parked facing the houses.

White nodded. "Fits our boys' MO. Any idea when?"

Jerry looked at White and smiled. "Trick or Treat."

"Halloween? You're sure?"

"What do you do when someone rings your doorbell on Halloween night?"

"I answer the door." White's eyes grew wide as he comprehended what Jerry was saying. "Oh, it can't be that simple."

Jerry winced as he twisted in the seat. "My feeling is your guys will hit all at once, just like you said. At a designated time, each man will ring the doorbell of whatever house number they've drawn, and it will be total chaos for the next three to five minutes. They will probably have alarms letting them know when to leave."

"You couldn't make it easy on me and tell me what houses, could you?"

"My guess is homes with double-door entrances. That's just a hunch. Check houses with large entryways. If I were looking to bust in a door, I would want one the owner couldn't block."

"I thought you'd said people will open the door."

"They will. But as soon as they discover the guys aren't kids, the owner will go on the defensive."

White looked out the window. "I see a flaw in your plan."

"What's that?"

"You just said it yourself. These guys aren't kids. I see a man standing at my door – I'm going to think twice about opening it."

"You don't think high schoolers go trick or treating? Besides, they will be in costumes."

"I don't suppose you know what kind of costumes?"

An image of the man he saw running across the field flashed into his mind. "Black costumes with glow-in-the-dark skeletons on the front." As soon as he said it, the last piece of the puzzle fell into place. Jerry hit the steering wheel. "Eureka!"

"Care to share your epiphany?"

"I'll do better than that. I'll show you." Jerry put the Durango in gear and did a U-turn. Instead of making a right out of the subdivision, he made a left. He pointed toward the side window. "What do you see over there?"

"A pond?"

"Besides that?"

White guessed again. "A field?"

Jerry smiled. "You're getting closer."

"I'd have worn my glasses if I'd known there'd be a quiz," White replied dryly.

"That is the toll road that leads into North Carolina."

White whistled his understanding.

Jerry continued. "Yesterday, when I was over here, I got a hit on a black SUV sitting on the side of 168. I didn't put two and two together at the time, but he was almost directly in line with where we are now." Jerry pointed. "Actually, he was just on the other side of that white sign over there. He was probably timing how long it would take someone to run across the field. There's a fence. They'll probably cut it. But that's how they are planning to make their escape. According to Max, these guys have guns."

"Max?"

"My partner." Jerry looked in the mirror when Gunter groaned. "Get comfortable, and I'll fill you in on the next part of the puzzle…"

***

Jerry stood outside of the courtroom waiting for Fred, who he'd yet to talk to since Rudy's interrogation. Max, April, Susie, and Savannah were inside, waiting for Rudy to be brought in for his arraignment.

The elevator dinged. Fred got off with a couple of men wearing suits. Fred saw Jerry and said something to the men, who continued into the courtroom.

Fred wiped at the bags under his eyes and faced Jerry. "We've agreed to a plea – before you lose your cool – we had no choice. The second Rudy started talking about the dog, we had to shut him down. The last thing we wanted was for him to live out his life in a psychiatric hospital where he would have a chance of being released."

Jerry ran a hand over his head. "What kind of plea?"

"Life in prison without parole in exchange for no needle and info on all his victims' whereabouts."

Jerry smiled. "I can agree to that."

Fred blew out a sigh. "I sure wish I knew what made you tick. I've been dreading telling you the whole morning. I drank about half a bottle of Maalox, thinking you'd jump up and down and tear the courthouse to shreds. Or worse, sic the dog on me. Where is he anyway?"

"If I know Gunter, he's tormenting our prisoner."

The elevator dinged, and Mario Fabel stepped off with two of his goons.

"What's he doing here?" Fred huffed.

"I called him."

"What? Are we, selling tickets now? This isn't a circus."

"Relax, Fred. Fabel has just as much right being here as anyone. Besides, his sister's inside."

Fred swallowed. "Ashley's here?"

"Yes, well, her spirit anyway."

"Jiminy Cricket."

Jerry shook his head. "He's not here. At least not that I know of, but the rest are."

Fred's face paled. "Rest."

"Patti O'Conner, Ashley Marie Fabel, Rita Wadsworth, Rosie Freeman, Fiona Johnson, and a few others that I didn't recognize. I'll work with them to find their bodies."

Fred's color was starting to return. "No need. Once the plea was reached, Rudy sang like a canary, giving us names, dates, and locations. The teams have been working all night to verify his claims. Also, turns out our guy really was a ghost or at least moved like one. He would walk into the hotel dressed in drag, which is why we never saw him on our cameras. I'm sure, now that we know, we'd find

Trudy, but that is why we never could find him."

"So he used a fake card to check into the hotel?"

"According to Rudy, he never paid for a hotel. He would walk right in through the front door like he belonged there. You know yourself most hotels never question who comes and goes. Sometimes, he'd go straight for the elevator. Others, he would head to the breakfast room. He'd eat breakfast and flirt with the businessmen. Can you imagine sitting on a commuter train and seeing Rudy's face next to a picture of him dressed as Trudy, then reading the article knowing you were one of the men duped? I don't feel so bad now. Anyway, he would hang around until he found someone who was leaving and borrow their room for a couple of hours."

Another piece of the puzzle fell into place. "That explains why I only got a hit near the bathroom. It was like the guy never even went near the bed."

"According to Rudy, it was easy to get a key recharged or simply approach the staff to request a clean set of sheets – which he used on the bed in his van."

Jerry remembered standing at the desk at the hotel in Niagara Falls, talking to the desk clerk, when a man stopped by the desk and asked for a set of sheets. Bryn, the clerk, had given the man a set without even asking which room they were for.

"Since most people leave without stopping by the front desk, he was able to slip into a room for a quick shower and then leave through the back entrance. He'd put his dirty sheets in a bag and drop them into the nearest maid cart for them to wash away the evidence, and no one was ever the wiser."

"No one ever questioned the blood?"

Fred shook his head. "I doubt they look at every set of sheets before they go into the wash. Pretty brilliant, if you think about it, although he still hasn't told us why."

"That's because he's hoping to sell his story and get rich off the public's need for drama."

"Probably. At least there won't be a long, drawn-out trial, which could lead to copycat killings."

The door opened, and Fabel stepped out into the hall. He caught Jerry's eye and nodded for him to come over.

"Looks like your friend wants to have a chat. Want me to stick around?"

Jerry shook his head. "No, Gunter and Ashley followed him out."

"Boy, you sure are something, McNeal."

"Yeah, maybe someday we'll find out what that something is." Jerry walked over to where Fabel was standing. "You wanted to talk?"

"Yeah, what's this about a plea bargain?"

The door opened, and a man stuck his head out. "It's starting."

Jerry wasn't all that interested in hearing the man's heinous crimes repeated, so he made no move to leave when Fabel stood his ground. "Listen, I just heard about it myself. Foster copped to all the murders and even gave up a few we didn't know about. The plea will keep him from getting off on an insanity plea."

"More like keep him from the needle," Fabel fumed. "The coward."

Jerry leaned back against the wall and crossed his arms. Gunter moved in between him and Fabel. "I thought you'd be happy there isn't going to be a trial."

Fabel narrowed his eyes. "Why should I be happy?"

"Because it will keep your sister's name out of the guy's mouth, and you won't have to look at his face when he sits there and gloats about everything he did to her."

"Yeah, I guess I can live with that. Especially when my guys get hold of him."

Ashley shook her head. "No, tell him this is not his fight. We want to be the ones to settle the score."

Jerry debated the wisdom of giving Fabel information he could use against him.

"Tell him, Jerry. I'll make him understand."

Fabel turned toward the courtroom. "Don't you want to see his face when the judge hands down the sentence?"

"No reason to. He already knows what's coming. Listen, I want you to reconsider putting a hit on the guy."

"Oh no you don't. We had an agreement. I let you find him, and I get to take care of him once he's on the inside. I upheld my end of the bargain. You don't get to protect the guy now." Fabel's nostrils flared, and Gunter emitted a low growl.

Jerry held up his hands. "I assure you I don't have any sympathy for the guy. Nor am I trying to protect him."

"Then what's your deal?"

Here goes nothing. "I'm not the one asking. Ashley is."

Fabel doubled up his fist. "My sister's killer is on the other side of that wall—Now's not the time to be playing with me, McNeal."

"I'm not playing with you. Ashley is here."

"I'm going to punch you right in the nose."

At least Fabel was a gentleman about it, which was less consideration than what Jerry had given to Foster.

Gunter moved to take Fabel's fist in his mouth, and Ashley beat him to it. She took her brother's hand and whispered something in his ear.

Though Jerry didn't hear what was said, he knew without a doubt that Ashley had just made a believer out of her brother.

Fabel's eyes grew wide as the color drained from his face. "You weren't lying. I knew you were hiding something. Holy crap, man, I can't believe she's really here."

"Are we good, Fabel?"

Sweat beaded on Mario's brow as he bobbed his head.

Jerry slipped into the courtroom just as the judge was announcing the sentence. To anyone else entering the room, it would look as if the right bench at the back of the room was free for the taking. But Jerry saw the truth. He was also aware when the spirit of each victim stood and followed Rudy Foster out of the room. The very last to leave was Patti O'Conner, who turned and blew him a kiss just before walking through the door.

***

Jerry opened the passenger door for April. "Are you sure you have to go?"

April got out and looked toward Max, who was kneeling and saying her goodbyes to Gunter. "Yes, Max has to get back to school. You know what they say? One needs to have a good education to land a good job."

Jerry chuckled. "I don't think Max has to worry about future employment."

April smiled. "No, but a girl should keep her options open."

Jerry looked her in the eye. "Does that go for the girl's mom?"

April's cheeks grew pink. "So, what's next for you? What does one do when not chasing a serial killer?"

"Go to the party capital of the world." Jerry winked. "At least that's what my parents tell me. They have a house in the Villages, Florida, and have been begging me to come for a visit. There are concerts every night and plenty of golf courses and swimming pools."

"Sounds fun. Do you even play golf?"

"Nope, but I think I could be rather adept at hanging around the swimming pool."

April kissed him on the cheek. "Thank you for saving my life, Jerry."

Jerry pulled her in for a hug. He felt her tremble. *Don't let her go, McNeal.*

"I've got to go." April pulled away. "Until next time, Jerry."

As soon as she started for the plane, Max ran over and threw her arms around him. "See ya, Jerry."

Jerry was taken aback. He thought for sure Max would have at least tried to get him to go with them. "Are you okay, Max?"

"Sure, why wouldn't I be?"

"No reason. Just making sure."

She leaned in and hugged him. "I know you have things to figure out, but I'm not worried."

"You're not? How come?"

"Because I know you love us."

"Of course, I care about both of you."

"I know you care. But I know you love us too."

"How can you be so sure?" *Especially when I'm not a hundred percent sure.*

"Because not only can I feel it here." Max pointed to her heart, then moved her finger to her forehead and smiled. "But I can see it here."

Jerry watched as she ran to the plane and raced up the rolling ladder that pressed against the white Learjet.

Gunter stood at the bottom of the ladder, barking as if asking her to return.

As the door closed behind her, Jerry had but one thought in his head. For as long as he'd known her, Max's feelings had never been wrong.

*Join Jerry McNeal and his ghostly
K-9 partner as they put their gifts to good use
in:*

Village Shenanigans
Book 11 in the Jerry McNeal series.

*Available November 29, 2022 on Amazon
Kindle:*

https://www.amazon.com/gp/product/B0BGSZ
26NY/

Please help me by leaving a review!

About the Author

Sherry A. Burton writes in multiple genres and has won numerous awards for her books. Sherry's awards include the coveted Charles Loring Brace Award, for historical accuracy within her historical fiction series, The Orphan Train Saga. Sherry is a member of the National Orphan Train Society, presents lectures on the history of the orphan trains, and is listed on the NOTC Speaker's Bureau as an approved speaker.

Originally from Kentucky, Sherry and her Retired Navy Husband now call Michigan home. Sherry enjoys traveling and spending time with her husband of more than forty years.